STINGRAY™

COMIC ANTHOLOGY
VOLUME TWO
BATTLE LINES

PART OF THE

STINGRAY™
DEADLY UPRISING
SAGA

Anderson Entertainment Limited
Third Floor, 86–90 Paul Street,
London, EC2A 4NE

Stingray Comic Anthology Volume Two: Battle Lines

Hardcover edition published by Anderson Entertainment in 2024.

Stingray ™ and © ITC Entertainment Group Limited, 1964, 2002 and 2024. Licensed by ITV Studios Limited.

Deadly Uprising ™ and © Anderson Entertainment 2024.

All Rights Reserved.

www.gerryanderson.com

All rights reserved. No part of this publication may be reproduced, stored in a retrieval system, or transmitted in any form or by any means, electronically, mechanical, photocopying, recording or otherwise, without the prior permission of the copyright owners and the publishers.

A CIP catalogue record for this book is available from the British Library

ISBN: 978-1-914522-72-7

Cover/Book Layout, Art and Strip Restoration:
Robert Hammond
Features Writer: Fred McNamara
Cover Art: Keith Burns
Art: Andrew Skilleter (pages 137, 235 and 283);
Keith Page (page 329)

With grateful thanks to:
Alan Grice, Paul Holder and Fred McNamara for loaning their comic collections.

Additional thanks to:
Andrew Skilleter
Keith Page
John Freeman
Ruth-Maria Hammond
Barnaby Eaton-Jones

Printed by: Atlas Book Solutions, Poland

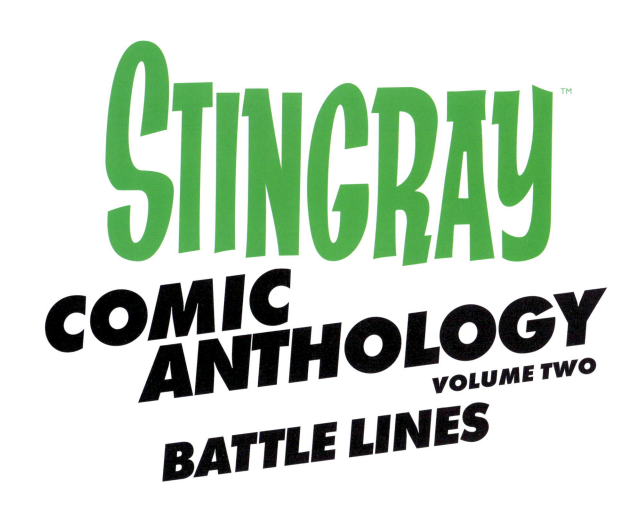

PART OF THE STINGRAY DEADLY UPRISING SAGA

ANDERSON ENTERTAINMENT

CONTENTS

In the year 2065, the World Aquanaut Security Patrol defends Earth from the villainous underwater despot Titan intent on taking over the terrainean world.

8   **Feature: Fugitive from Marineville**

12   **Marineville Traitor**
Issues #155–#189
Artist: Michael Strand / Jon Davies.
Troy becomes a hunted fugitive when he's framed for the destruction of a World Navy bomber. Stealing Stingray before his imprisonment, Tempest embarks on a globe-trotting mission of vengeance to clear his name and uncovers an elaborate plot to destroy Marineville from within.

    High Treason (#155–#157)
    The Circle of Liros (#158–#168)
    The Black Museum (#169–#171)
    The Law of Bulasaki (#172–#176)
    Trench of Destruction (#177–#181)
    Tempest's Revenge (182–#189)

83   **Introduction #2: Commander Shore**
Commander Shore shares vital information in his Priority Update on the Deadly Uprising.

84   **Desperate Measures**
Writer: Andrew Clements.
Artist: Neil Roberts.
Letterer: Emily Joyce Stewart.
The Stingray team travels to several undersea cities seeking to forge new alliances against Titan's growing assault fleet. While some races join them willingly, others prove more difficult to convince.

90   **Feature: Stingray's Special Extras**

94   **Double Trap**
TV Century 21 Stingray Special
Artist: Ron Turner.
Maniacal marine biologist Dr Francis Holbien lures the Stingray crew into a trap to add the W.A.S.P. submarine to his collection of underwater treasures.

98   **The Big Freeze**
TV Century 21 Stingray Special
Artist: Ron Embleton.
The freezing of the cargo liner Northern Star sends Stingray into battle against the Atlantises race who plot to freeze the terrainean world.

102   **Titan's Revenge**
TV Century 21 Stingray Special
(*Marina, Girl of the Sea*)
Artist: Unknown.
Marina witnesses an armada of Terror Fish lead by Titan launching an attack on the underwater city Equapol. Warning the city of their imminent danger, Equapol strikes back against Titan's forces but in revenge he captures Marina to be his slave

106   **Aquaphibian Attack**
TV Century 21 Summer Extra 1965
Artist: Ron Embleton.
A pair of Aquaphibians succeed in rendering Stingray's radio waves useless and accompany the W.A.S.P. vessel into Marineville undetected to destroy the base from within.

110 Deadly Ceremony

TV Century 21 International Extra 1965

Artist: Ron Embleton.

On investigating tremendous activity emanating from Titanica, Troy, Phones and Marina stumble upon a deadly underwater ritual.

115 The Volcano

TV Century 21 International Extra 1965

Artist: Ron Turner.

A trio of scientists evacuate from the erupting Mount Mosoto leaving behind their valuable Delta Computer in their panic-stricken state. Stingray has just three-and-a-half hours to rescue the device before Marineville bombards the unstoppable volcanic eruption with hydromic missiles.

122 Tentacles of Terror

TV Century 21 Summer Extra 1966

Artist: Michael Strand.

Stingray comes to the rescue of a deep-sea drilling bell with a two-man crew trapped inside that's been captured by a giant octopus.

126 The Underwater Dragon

Lady Penelope Summer Extra 1966

(Marina, Girl of the Sea)

Artist: Rab Hamilton.

A fierce underwater dragon threatens a neighbouring city near Pacifica but Marina braves the creature's outburst when she discovers the reason for its fury.

128 Tempus Fugit

Writer: Nick Abadzis.

Artist: Simon Fraser.

While seeking an alliance with the shadowy, sand-like Silicanans, Troy is subjected to a truth-divining process to gauge his true motivations. X-20's arrival puts Troy's impassioned plea in jeopardy.

134 Feature: How the Beautiful and Mysterious Marina May Never Speak Again

138 World of Silence

Issues #1–#23

Artist: Rab Hamilton.

The peaceful existence of the beautiful underwater girl Marina and her father Aphony, ruler of the underwater paradise of Pacifica, is shattered by the warmongering Titan when he lays waste to the city. Marina, Aphony and his first minister Barinth embark on a string of jeopardous adventures to escape Titan, but Titan is saving his cruellest assault until the very end.

161 The Thoughtful Gift

Issues #24–#32

Artist: Rab Hamilton.

In the wake of their silenced lives, Marina and Aphony discover they can still communicate via thought transference. To test how strong their newfound powers are, Marina hunts out an artefact from a faraway sunken temple as a present for her father. However, when a giant killer squid captures Marina, the father and daughter's abilities are put to the ultimate test.

170 Aphony's Masterplan

Issues #33–#47

Artist: Rab Hamilton.

When Titan attacks the underwater city of Vincta, Aphony discovers that his and Marina's mental powers can overthrow Titan's Aquaphibian armada. Enraged, Titan captures Marina to be his slave so that Aphony will be forced never to use his powers again. But with Titan unable to read the Pacificans' thoughts himself, he and Aphony attempt to outwit each other as a dangerous plan is hatched to rescue Marina.

185 Danger at Oceanis

Issues #48–#52

Artist: Rab Hamilton.

Marina and Aphony visit the reclusive nation of Oceanis to establish a union of goodwill but are warned by the Oceanians of a rogue dog-shark that's on the loose. However, when the dog-shark rescues Marina from a landslide, the hostile forces feared by the Oceanians may be closer to home.

190 Staria's Betrayal

Issues #53–#60

Artist: Rab Hamilton.

Titan forces his prisoner niece Staria to spy on Oceanis so that he may overthrow the nation and abuse its wealth and resources for his own ends. In return for her freedom, she must kill the Oceanian King, Marina and Aphony.

198 The Healing Weed

Issues #61–#69

Artist: Rab Hamilton.

Marina's search for a special weed which can cure a gravely ill Aphony results in the primitive yet violent Gormog race to mistakenly believe that they're under attack. Marina must use all her cunning to foil an invasion of Pacifica by the Gormogs, which involves calling upon the one person who can save them – Titan!

207 Ceremony of Neptunius

Issues #70–#78

Artist: Colin Andrew.

The jewel of Neptunius, a precious talisman that's passed down to the heir of Pacifica, is stolen by the Pacifican child Leoni. When searching for her, Marina and Leoni are captured by the slave trader Targax. Marina's desperate plans for escape results in Targax selling them both to Titan.

216 Bride of Boldar

Issues #79–#84

Artist: Colin Andrew.

When King Voltis is caught in a violent landslide, his dying wish is for his obnoxious son and Marina to marry. Aghast at her future as Boldar's wife, Marina is forced to choose between escaping her fate and rescuing Boldar when his life becomes threatened by the eruption of an underwater volcano.

222 Escape from Titanica

Issues #85–#88

Artist: Colin Andrew.

Marina is captured and made Titan's slave when she's caught in the crossfire between Titan's Terror Fish and the World Security Patrol submarine Sea Probe. When the

W.A.S.P. vessel Stingray investigates and is subsequently captured by Titan, Marina helps Troy and Phones make their escape.

226 Rescue in the Depths

Writer: Nick Abadzis.

Artist: Simon Fraser.

X-20 seizes an opportunity to capture Troy and return him to Titanica in order to regain Titan's favour. Troy discovers in the domain of the Silicanans, reality isn't all that it appears to be.

232 Feature: Countdown to Stingray

236 Terror of Titan

Issue #3

Artist: Michael Strand.

Stingray is tasked with protecting the computerized Sea Slug submarine on its mission to stabilize a series of gargantuan underwater tremors that risk sending huge tidal waves crashing into Earth's coastlines. However, Titan aims to sabotage the mission.

242 The Cyber Saboteurs

Issues #6–#11

Artist: Michael Strand.

Marineville allows Professor Morrison to hunt for rare fossils on W.A.S.P. grounds. However, the professor is secretly working for an enemy organization seeking to overthrow the W.A.S.P.s by replacing its members with cyber-controlled doppelgangers.

254 Polar Peril

Issue #13

Artist: Colin Page.

The trigger-happy Captain Hail of the World Navy risks starting an undersea war when he disobeys Commander Shore's orders and pilots the Sea Dragon against the Polarian race.

260 The Waters of Hyde

Issues #15–#21

Artist: Michael Strand / Rab Hamilton.

Stingray is dispatched to Mars to investigate the disappearance of a survey team who were investigating a newly discovered ocean beneath the Martian surface. Troy and Phones soon discover a race of cave dwellers, and water that transforms them into violent ape-men.

274 Model Mission
Issue #22
Artist: Brian Lewis.
An enemy from Phones's past succeeds in destroying W.A.S.P. vessels Thornback and Barracuda, and Phones and Stingray are next on the villain's list.

280 Feature: The Fleetway Years

284 How It All Began
Issue #4
Artist: Steve Kyte.
The oceans of the world are kept at peace thanks to the efforts of the W.A.S.P.s, but the super submarine Stingray soon encounters the villainous despot Titan and his beautiful slave girl, Marina.

286 Plant of Doom
Issues #5–#7
Artist: John Cooper.
In the wake of Marina's alignment with the W.A.S.P.s, Titan hatches a deadly scheme of revenge involving a seemingly beautiful flower that exudes a dangerous scent. When the plant ends up in Marineville, Marina is accused of attempting to murder Atlanta.

295 Hostages of the Deep
Issues #8–#10
Artist: John Cooper.
Former W.A.S.P. alumni Admiral Carson and his wife Millie have their idyllic island retirement ruined when they're captured by the villainous Gadus. Marina attempts to rescue the Carsons herself, but becomes entrapped by Gadus.

304 Triple Cross
Writer: James Swallow.
Artist: Connor Flanagan.
A final council of war is held with the assembled representatives of each of Titan's allies. The Solarstar reveal their true intentions and attack Titan's forces. But Titan is prepared for their treachery.

310 The Big Gun
Issues #11–#13
Artist: John Cooper.
The Solarstar race launches an unstoppable onslaught against several Pacific islands. Stingray's pursuit of the Solarstar's missile-firing craft sends them into ocean depths of such fantastic pressures that Troy and Phones lose consciousness before they can stop the aliens.

319 The Ghost Ship
Issues #14–#16
Artist: Nigel Parkinson.
The jetliner Arcadia is destroyed by a ghostly galleon. Investigating the ancient sailing ship, Commander Shore and Phones are captured by its alien pilot, who demands that Troy be imprisoned for his crimes against underwater civilizations.

330 Feature: Stingray's Fun Days

332 The Orange Cloud
Issues #156–#177
Artist: Keith Page.
Titan attacks Troy with a mysterious chemical weapon which causes Stingray to attract ferocious sea creatures.

352 Night Raid
Issues #178–#185
Artist: Keith Page.
Troy, Phones, Marina and Atlanta have an evening's celebrations interrupted when Titan launches an army of mechanical crabs to destroy Marineville.

360 Battle for Marineville
Writer: Ernie Altbacker.
Artist: Lee Sullivan.
Colourist: Connor Flanagan.
Letterer: Emily Joyce Stewart.
The final battle begins! Stingray, totally outclassed by the deadly Orca under Titan's command, must prove that the human spirit and ingenuity can triumph over even the most impossible odds.

FEATURE
FUGITIVE FROM MARINEVILLE

Stingray in TV Century 21, 1968

In January 1968, issue #155 of *TV Century 21* (renamed *TV21* from issue #156) saw the comic undergo one of its most drastic overhauls yet. The newly launched *Captain Scarlet and the Mysterons* strip, having blasted off in the comic's centre pages in time for the debut of the television series in late September 1967, now firmly occupied the comic's first few pages – meaning that *TV Century 21*'s famous tabloid-styled front cover was retooled to make room for the first page of that week's *Captain Scarlet* strip. The double-page centre spread, once a hallmark of a strip's status in *TV Century 21*, was abandoned entirely to allow the comic to be a more attractive prospect for international translations.

Aside from this cosmetic change the *Captain Scarlet* strip would continue, along with regular heavyweights *Thunderbirds* and *Zero X*. But for several of the comic's former champions, changes were significantly more severe. Brent Cleever was transported out of the 'past' of the 2040s and brought out of retirement to become the superhero Mr. Magnet, abandoning his Universal Secret Service roots. The *Fireball XL5* strip, having already been reduced from the full-bloodied colours of Mike Noble to a black-and-white strip shared between Don Lawrence, Tom Kerr and Colin Andrew, was now adjusted still further to a text feature, lasting until issue #167 before being permanently retired.

The *Stingray* strip, by comparison, was allowed a more ambitious finale. Issue #154 features the only standalone *Stingray* story ever to be published by the comic, if we discount *Stingray*'s involvement in The Astran War. Once this brief tale was out of the way, issue #155 began a hugely dramatic, extravagantly lengthy serial that saw Captain Troy Tempest framed for the destruction of the strike bomber craft TLR 20. Escaping his court martial, Troy steals Stingray and embarks on a mission across the world's oceans to clear his name and uncover the truth behind the attack. His adventures take him across Japan, Egypt, Malaysia, Australia and Greece. What he eventually discovers is a complicated, prolonged plan to devastate

(above) The cover of *TV21* issue #155, from January 1968

Marineville from within by enemies who seek to unravel the harmonious set-up of the World Security Patrol.

Marineville Traitor ran for a staggering 34 issues, running between January and August of 1968. The serial is made up of several shorter stories, each leading into the events of the other, as Troy's perilous efforts to uncover clues as to the identity and motives of his enemies build momentum, each revelation leading to the next fresh mini-adventure. The episodes themselves can be enjoyed individually in the issues as follows: *High Treason* (#155–#157), *The Circle of Liros* (#158–#168), *The Black Museum* (#169–#171), *The Law of Bulasaki* (#172–#176), *Trench of Destruction* (#177–#181) and *Tempest's Revenge* (#182–#189). This serial boasts the globe-trotting sense of scale of a classic *Asterix the Gaul* adventure, whilst throwing forward to the multi-episode arcs of *Judge Dredd* from *2000 AD*. Throughout the serial, Troy and later Phones (who allies with his friend at the risk of his own life), encounter violent crab-like underwater aliens, maniacal scientists and crazed super-villains. A revolving line-up of villains increases the sense of scale and momentum that the serial builds, before revealing its true antagonists in time for the riotous finale.

Multiple writers and editors are associated with this hugely prolonged epic. The serial came about under the brief tenure of the lesser-known editor Chris Spencer, but it's more likely that either script editors Angus Allan or Richard O'Neill instigated the serial, and therefore likely contributed to it. O'Neill himself is perhaps best known for writing two of the five *Captain Scarlet* audio dramas alongside the more well-recognised Allan. We may presume that Dennis Hooper would still have been writing on the *Stingray* strip at this point – he, Allan, Tod Sullivan and Howard Elson were with the comic from beginning to its end. Early on in the strip, Troy follows the trail of a mysterious medallion left at the scene of the bomber's attack, a plot device that had been utilised in the much earlier adventure *The Medallion Mystery*, a storyline itself attributed to Hooper. Evidence of his contribution by recycling ideas, perhaps?

Surviving scripts show that regular freelancer Scott Goodall contributed the Japanese-centric episodes, and they do indeed boast his rather characteristic sensationalist flair for storytelling. It's quite probable that the fourth storyline, *Trench of Destruction*, also came from Goodall, given how similar they are. Both storylines involve wannabe dictators hatching outlandish plots to overthrow Eastern cultures for their own nefarious means, including both using robotic weaponry. Quite tellingly, neither storyline is substantially linked to the larger fugitive adventure at work. These 'interlude' episodes may have also been beneficial for working out just how exactly the serial was going to end! The episodes can also be taken as evidence of multiple writers at work on the overall serial and therefore perhaps not entirely working to the same brief.

Michael Strand remained on artistic duties until issue #176, after which Jon Davies picked the strip up for its last 12 installments. Strand would go on to draw the *Joe 90* strip in *Joe 90: Top Secret* and even return to *Stingray* territory for *Countdown* in the early 1970s. Strand was also an irregular presence throughout Gerry Anderson annuals of the late 1960s and early 1970s, contributing to the 1970 *TV21* annual, the 1967 and 1972 *Thunderbirds* annuals, and the *Project S.W.O.R.D.* annual.

(above) The cover of *TV21* issue #176, from June 1968

The grandeur of *Marineville Traitor* was rather dampened by the strip's shift in format. Having already shifted into monochrome, the *Stingray* strip was cut back still further from being a two-page strip to now functioning as a page-and-a-half. This format had to be adjusted accordingly when the serial was reprinted in Fleetway Editions' *Stingray Monthly* and later *The New Thunderbirds* in the early 1990s. The artwork would now be fully colourised and numerous cliffhanger panels were shaved from various installments so that several chapters could be slotted into a single issue to keep a smooth flow.

Strand's characteristically expressive artwork remains in solid form throughout his tenure on the serial, emphasising the danger that Troy is constantly thrown into. However, the scaled-back nature of the strip's format results in Strand's action sequences feeling undeniably smothered. Davies feels more at home with the condensed nature of this long-running adventure. Joining the strip around June 1968, Davies was fresh off of illustrating *The Angels* in the pages of *Lady Penelope*, a strip he'd singlehandedly illustrated since January 1967.

Marineville Traitor even fed into story material outside of the comic. The 1969 *TV21* annual carries the standalone *Stingray* comic story *Invisible Death* in which the fugitive Troy stumbles upon a plot by Titan to use undetectable, heat-seeking jellyfish to destroy Marineville. Troy decides to surrender himself to Commander Shore in the hopes of warning him of the impending destruction, but his warning falls on deaf ears. Only with the help of Phones can Troy hope to save Marineville.

The 1969 *TV21* annual would have been released around September/October time of 1968 – intriguingly just as *Marineville Traitor* would have been coming to its end. This brief four-page adventure, illustrated by John Cooper, shows Troy piloting Stingray alone. This story has therefore to take place early on within the events of *Marineville Traitor*, prior to the Japanese-set episodes during which Phones decides to partner with Troy and aid him in proving his innocence. Comic annuals were regularly released around September or October in time for the Christmas season, but they were prepared much earlier in the year, which would explain this story's peculiar presence in relation to the main strip itself.

Marineville Traitor may lack some of the sharply tuned focus of *Stingray*'s lengthier serials under Alan Fennell, but it remains one of the strip's grandest efforts. Rather than rely entirely on other, more popular Anderson strips to continue to carry the comic's creative success into its final years, *TV21*'s editors and writers saw fit to rejuvenate the comic's old line-up in engrossingly unpredictable ways. *Marineville Traitor* marks the end of *Stingray*'s 189-issue run in *TV Century 21/TV21* and climaxes on a rousing note as Troy succeeds in proving his innocence, outing the perpetrators and exposing their deceit before Marineville can be devastated. A triumphant end to one of *TV21*'s lengthiest and most enduring efforts, and the comic's *Stingray* strip in general.

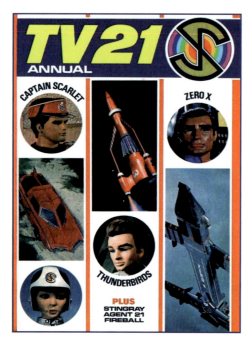

(above) The cover of *TV21* Annual 1969

CORGI MODEL CLUB NEWS

A MODEL CLUB MEMBERSHIP FORM WITH EVERY CORGI MODEL

DAKTARI

DAKTARI (Swahili for doctor) is an exciting world wide television adventure series about a warm-hearted and courageous scientist dedicated to preserving wild life in the African Jungle.

He lives with his gay teen-age daughter and two assistants and has two strange pets—Clarence, a cross-eyed bespectacled lion, and a mischievous and highly intelligent chimp named Judy. His constant battle is against cruel and lawless men killing for the sake of killing or who traffic in hide, ivory and captive beasts.

Stars of this series both animal and human are seen in the pictures on this page. Clarence, the lion is getting a medical check over from Dr. Marsh Tracy (played by Marshall Thompson), and on the left Enid, the Giraffe, gets the beauty treatment from Yale Summers who plays Jack Dane in the series. Top right, all the stars of Daktari with the exception of Clarence are together—in the front Judy the Chimp, then Marshall Thompson with friend Toto on his shoulders, Yale Summers and Cheryl Miller behind.

Corgi Gift Set 7 Daktari

CORGI MODEL CLUB NEWS

A MODEL CLUB MEMBERSHIP FORM WITH EVERY CORGI MODEL

The GREEN HORNET

BLACK BEAUTY

Here is a story direct from the television screen of the U.S.A. It is the saga of Britt Reid, the famous American newspaper editor by day, 'The Green Hornet' waging war against crime by night. These are the dual roles of this exciting hero who, to complete the mystery surrounding his identity, permits himself to be considered a ruthless criminal in some quarters to serve as a cover-up for his crime-fighting activities.

'Black Beauty', famous automobile of 'The Green Hornet', is equipped with a variety of fantastic gadgets. They include a button-operated camera with a focussing range of four miles, closed circuit TV and apparatus which spreads a film of ice behind the car to foil pursuers.

However, the Corgi model of this fantastic car includes the most spectacular features: the car itself is a large, black sedan, with green purdah glass all round, to conceal the occupants. The Green Hornet himself is in the rear seat, sweeping an effective arc of fire with his tear-gas pistol. At the wheel is his assistant Kato, expert driver and practitioner of Gung-Fu, an advanced form of Karate and ju-jitsu. On the textured roof of the model is the emblem of The Green Hornet. The radiator grille looks innocent enough but at the touch of a lever the grille lowers and discharges an immobilising missile at the fleeing bandits. Also revealed are the simulated battery of squirt guns on either side of the grille. Another notable surprise in the Corgi model is discovered when the second lever is released, for the boot-lid opens and a radar scanner flies through the air.

From the illustrations on this page you will see how cleverly Corgi have reproduced the real vehicle (top right and left) in this new exciting model (bottom pictures). As with all Corgi Crime Busters' vehicles, secret instructions for owners are concealed in the base of the plinth on which the model stands.

CORGI MODEL CLUB news

A MODEL CLUB MEMBERSHIP FORM WITH EVERY CORGI MODEL

BIG BROTHER

YOU may have noticed that there is a new Lotus Elan on the roads nowadays. Or perhaps you have not noticed, because it is very similar in appearance to the Lotus Elan which has been in production for the last few years and which is available in several versions as a Corgi model, with a detachable chassis in coupe form, or as an open two-seater. The new version is made only as a closed coupe. It is also much larger than the earliest version, with an overall length greater by 2 ft., and an overall width increased by 10 in. This means that the new version—called the Lotus Elan + 2, by the way—is quite a big car, while the original one was not only small in overall dimensions, but looked tiny, because of its perfect proportions. The biggest surprise of the plus 2 however, is that it has two extra seats, hence the name, so that four people can ride in Lotus style and comfort—the first time this has ever been possible in a Lotus. The two versions are shown side by side in the top picture with Lotus chief, Colin Chapman between them.

The Lotus Elan plus 2 is even smoother than the original Elan, and it has inboard retractable headlights.

The increased length of the Lotus Elan plus 2 has resulted in even sleeker lines and yet there is room for two more passengers.

Corgi's Lotus Elan coupe has a detachable chassis.

CORGI MODEL CLUB NEWS

A MODEL CLUB MEMBERSHIP FORM WITH EVERY CORGI MODEL

THE MOTOR CAR—5
TRANSMISSION AND GEARBOX

Though the petrol engine is clearly the most efficient type of power unit for cars, special problems do arise in transmitting its power to the road. Unlike the electric motor and the steam engine, the petrol engine gives very little power at low revolutions and only produces its best power within a very narrow speed range. A gearbox is necessary to enable the engine to be run at its best power and speed to suit the driving conditions. We have illustrated here various engine locations (left), a typical layout (bottom left) and, below, the gearbox.

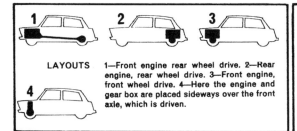

LAYOUTS 1—Front engine rear wheel drive. 2—Rear engine, rear wheel drive. 3—Front engine, front wheel drive. 4—Here the engine and gear box are placed sideways over the front axle, which is driven.

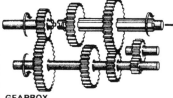

GEARBOX
The gearbox relies on the simple mechanics of toothed gearing—a small gear wheel will turn a larger wheel with more teeth more slowly but more powerfully. A large wheel will turn a smaller one faster but with less power. Thus, the power of the engine can be transmitted by the gearbox to give more power at less speed or more speed with less power at the road wheels. Above right—first gear, left, second gear.

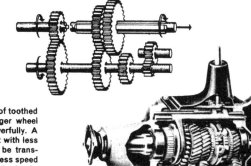

A TYPICAL LAYOUT Until fairly recently the majority of cars had front mounted engines with rear wheel drive. From this skeleton layout below follow the train of power from the engine, through the clutch to the gearbox, along the propeller shaft to the differential which transmits the power through 90 degrees via the rear axle, to the rear wheels.

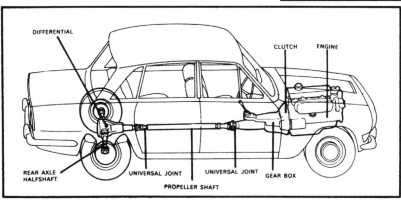

Corgi Model of the Lancia Fulvia Sport Zagato—1300 c.c. front mounted engine driving the front wheels.

CORGI MODEL CLUB NEWS

CLUB MEMBERSHIP FORM WITH EVERY CORGI MODEL

Denis Hulme and Chris Amon at the Dutch Grand Prix.

DENIS HULME WORLD CHAMP

New Zealand racing driver, Denis Hulme won the World Championship in 1967 driving a Repco-Brabham formula 1 car. He won the two toughest races of the year—the round-the-houses battle at Monaco, and the mountainous German Grand Prix on the Nurburgring. He was 'Rookie of the Year' at Indianapolis, a coveted award for the best new driver at the 'Brickyard'. Suddenly success has hit Denny Hulme, but it hasn't changed him. He is still the quiet, casual, New Zealander who arrived in England for the first time eight years ago and started his first race with a Cooper at Silverstone, driving in his bare feet! He said then that he gained a better 'feel' of the pedals...

Denny Hulme started racing almost by accident. He owned an MG TF sports car in New Zealand, competing in a few club races and hillclimbs. Soon he was racing a later model MG 'A'. Eventually, he traded his MG for a single-seater 2000c.c. Cooper-Climax and immediately started making a name for himself. He won the 'Driver to Europe' award in 1960, which was a form of motor racing 'scholarship' and he came to England to try his hand. For a time he worked in Jack Brabham's garage, servicing customers' cars.

The 1966 season was his first full year in formula 1 and he used it to learn the circuits, and to get used to the power of the 3-litre Repco V8 engine. One year later he was World Champion.

The lad in this picture proudly looking at his Corgi model of the Cooper-Maserati Formula 1 racing car is only 5 years old. What will the cars look like when he is old enough to compete in Grand Prix racing?

Denis Hulme leading the field at Nurburgring and, below, competing in the French Grand Prix.

CORGI MODEL CLUB NEWS

A MODEL CLUB MEMBERSHIP FORM WITH EVERY CORGI MODEL

Each year sees the introduction of new 'way out' cars. Not all survive the rigorous testing that is necessary before they reach the public. Others are regarded by the manufacturers as mobile test-beds in themselves, the basis of practical research into engine development and aerodynamics.

Here we present a selection of cars which made their first appearance in 1967. (top left) Town car of the future? The Ford Electric for the commuter. (below) The Italian Os Silver Fox: the driver sits in the offside nacelle; the engine is mounted in the other. Current engine of this car is of 1,000 c.c. capacity, but there are big possibilities for future development. in the record-attempt field.

On the right we display the Ghia line: (top) the 418 h.p. Ford-engined Mangusta and the Corgi model of the Ghia L6.4. At the bottom of the page two contrasts from Maserati: the 175 m.p.h. Ghibli coupe and below it, the Corgi model of the Cooper-Maserati V-2 Formula I racing car.

ODD CARS

CORGI MODEL CLUB NEWS
A MODEL CLUB MEMBERSHIP FORM WITH EVERY CORGI MODEL

Becoming a Car Stylist

Trevor Fioré

TVR Tina Coupe drawing.

Tina Spider drawing.

(Below) Tina Coupe at London Motor Show

Corgi Model No. 340 1967 Monte Carlo Sunbeam Imp.

Motor shows provide specialised designers with the opportunity to show their skills in making dream cars, or possibly promising prototypes. One young man who is fast making a reputation for himself in this field is Trevor Fioré.

He was born in Paris; his father is English; his mother French; and his grandfather Italian. At three, during the war, he was sent to England. At school, like most boys, he drew cars and all sorts of vehicles and remembers designing streamlined tram cars at ten years of age!

Having trained at the fabulous Pininfarina in Turin, he is now a consultant stylist with another company near Turin, Fissore. Last year he became interested in the little Hillman Imp and he took what is a functional and popular little rear engined saloon and turned it into a sleek coupe. When his special Imp, the Tina, was shown at the Paris show he received a blank cheque on opening day from a Frenchman who wanted to buy the car there and then. In London, where he showed an open version of the car, more people wanted to buy his creations, and when the show closed Trevor Fioré had been launched.

At 30 years of age he has about five years of designing behind him. To budding young designers he says 'You need to develop a sound engineering knowledge and combine it with your budding artistic talents.'

CORGI MODEL CLUB news

A MODEL CLUB MEMBERSHIP FORM WITH EVERY CORGI MODEL

THE MOTOR CAR—6
DIFFERENTIAL AND STEERING

DIFFERENTIAL

When a car is turning a corner, the outer rear wheel travels further than the inner and rotates faster to cover a greater distance. The differential gear of the driving axle makes allowances for the different distances covered by the wheels, accelerating the outer wheel and greatly reducing the risk of skidding. In a conventional design in which the engine is at the front, driving through a clutch and gearbox to the rear axle, the differential transmits the drive through a right angle to the two half-shafts. A hypoid gear in which the pinion on the end of the propeller shaft is set below the centre of the crown wheel is most popular today because it allows the shaft tunnel to be made lower. Transverse-engined cars, such as the BMC Mini, do not require a right-angle drive gear.

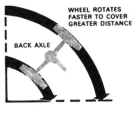

WHY IT'S NEEDED
When cornering, the outer rear wheel of a car travels further and faster than the inner. The differential (below left) achieves this.

STEERING

In producing an efficient steering gear for a car designers are obliged to come to a compromise with the different requirements of accuracy, lightness and sensitivity. A car which steered like a bicycle would be uncontrollable at high speed. Steering geared to be really 'feather-light' may lack 'feel' and be inaccurate in cornering. The systems used on the modern car are aimed at providing high accuracy, reasonable lightness both in parking and high speed driving and freedom from shocks transmitted from the road wheels to the driver's hands. The most usual form of steering gear employs special mechanism at the bottom to transmit movement to each wheel individually through links and rods. In some cases a worm gear moves a peg up and down, a drop-arm passing the movement to the drag-link. In the rack and pinion system a gear-wheel moves a rack on the track-rod from side to side. Many large cars today are equipped with power-steering to reduce the amount of effort required in manoeuvring at low speed. This is a hydraulic arrangement in which fluid power is fed into the system in proportion to the force applied at the steering wheel. Parking and cornering are equally effortless.

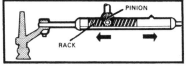

Rack and Pinion: Perhaps the most accurate and direct system today. A pinion moves a rack from side to side.

Worm and Peg: The most common steering system for British cars. The worm moves a peg up and down.

Recirculatory Ball: This is a smoother, more refined type of the worm and peg steering gear system

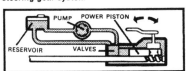

Power Steering: A hydraulic system which feeds its power to the steering linkage in proportion to the effort applied at the wheel.

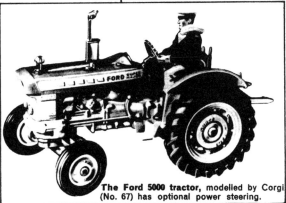

The Ford 5000 tractor, modelled by Corgi (No. 67) has optional power steering.

OUT OF THE FRYING PAN...

CORGI MODEL CLUB NEWS

A MODEL CLUB MEMBERSHIP FORM WITH EVERY CORGI MODEL

DAYTONA 500

Imagine riding in a saloon car at three times the legal speed limit. Imagine that it's got an engine seven times as big as a Mini. Imagine that in it you can average 180 miles an hour around a 2½ mile oval circuit.

Frightening, isn't it?

But that's what the Daytona 500 race is all about. Run at Daytona Beach in Florida it is the fastest and most exciting race in the world. And that is no hollow boast for the winner of last year's event ran at an average speed for the total 500 miles of 160.6 m.p.h. The fastest man to qualify for the race was Curtis Turner driving a Chevelle at 180.8 m.p.h. The race, which provides almost unheard of prize money for the winners, is for what the Americans call stock cars. Unlike the British version of stock cars these are in fact normal American family saloons. Fords, Dodges, Plymouths, Chevrolets, 50 of them take the start in this exciting race which is an annual event in the February of every year. Many of the cars have engines of 7 litres, seven times the size of the normal British mini.

The regulations permit the owners to make minor modifications to the engine and bodywork of the cars. But the modifications are limited for the object of the race is to prove to the American public which car is the fastest and toughest.

Over 90,000 people turned up to watch last year's race and see the massive cars rumbling along the straights at close to 200 m.p.h. and watch them run through the bends rubbing the bodywork, door to door, hub cap to hub cap. How's that for drama!

Typical American Stock Car and Hot Rod meeting.

American Stock Cars are covered with advertising slogans.

How does the driver see out of windows plastered like these with Op-art decorations?

There's no superfluous weight in this stock car. Hence the name!

Here is Corgi's own version of the Chevrolet Stingray in American Stock Car form.

CORGI MODEL CLUB NEWS

A MODEL CLUB MEMBERSHIP FORM WITH EVERY CORGI MODEL

Pat Moss (Lancia), winner of the Ladies prize.

Vic Elford and D. Stone (Porsche), outright winners.

T. Fall and M. Wood (Mini-Cooper) fourth overall.

1968 MONTE CARLO RALLY WINNERS

Every newcomer to rally driving nurses the ambition to drive in the classic Monte Carlo Rally. With starting points all over Europe, the worst winter weather can be confidently expected. Wet, cobbled roads, snow and ice, and most feared of all, fog, call for skill and nerve of the highest order. There was drama in the final stages this year when the leader, Larousse (Renault Alpine) crashed on snow shovelled on to the road by spectators. Close behind were the final winners, the British crew, Elford and Stone (Porsche) who swept past to victory. Their Finnish team-mates Toivonen and Tinkkanen were second, Aaltonen and Liddon came third in a Mini-Cooper and the Ladies prize went to Pat Moss-Carlsson and Elizabeth Nystrom in a Lancia Fulvia.

P. Hopkirk and R. Crellin (Mini-Cooper) finished fifth.

And Corgi collectors have all the winners! (Extreme left), the Zagato model of the Lancia Fulvia; (left) The Porsche Carrera 6 in Le Mans trim, with hinged tail unit giving access to the engine; (Right) 1967 Monte Carlo Mini, snow tyres on the roof and a battery of six lamps.

CORGI MODEL CLUB news

A MODEL CLUB MEMBERSHIP FORM WITH EVERY CORGI MODEL

THE MOTOR CAR-7
SUSPENSION AND SHOCK ABSORBERS

The suspension system of the modern car is a compromise by the designer. His problem is to give the car comfort, stability and safe road-holding under all normal conditions at an acceptable price. Soft passenger seats are not enough to ensure comfort. The car must absorb road shocks and roll and pitch have to be controlled. Moreover, the suspension requirements of a family car are quite different from those of a sports or racing car. All modern cars have independent front suspension, each wheel moving individually and remaining at right angles to the road. Most cars have non-independent rear suspension because it is a relatively simple arrangement, efficient for all normal motoring purposes and is inexpensive. Where cost is no object and very high speeds are involved, rear independent suspension systems exist to improve road-holding, cornering power and comfort.

FRONT SUSPENSION

Wishbone: The most widely used type. Parallel links of unequal length swing in a lateral arc. Springing is usually by longitudinal torsion bar or coil.

Macpherson Strut: Used on several Ford models. A bottom wishbone with the wheel attached to an inclined telescopic strut follows a large arc laterally. Coil springing.

Swing Axle: The type used in the rear-engined Rootes cars. Swing links follow arc longitudinally. The wheel is at a right angle to a stub axle hinged near the centre line of the coil spring.

Trailing Link: As used on the Volkswagen and Citroen. Swing links follow arc longitudinally. Track constant but wheelbase varies. Torsion bars or liquid springs.

REAR SUSPENSION

Live: Usually mounted on longitudinal leaf springs of thickness and length to suit the car. Sometimes controlled by trailing links or a Panhard rod. The spring leaves are sometimes separated by rubber or permanently greased.

Independent: Many different systems are in use today. Jaguar favour double wishbones. Triumph and Ford use semi-trailing link, B.M.C. and Citroen employ trailing link for their front-wheel drive cars. High cornering power, and improved comfort.

Swing Axle: The simplest form of independent rear suspension and a feature of most rear-engined cars. Although the system is simple and reliable it does create big differences in track and wheel angle.

De Dion: Combines all the best features of independent and non-independent systems. The unsprung weight is low but the De Dion system maintains a constant track and keeps the wheels at right angles to the road.

SHOCK ABSORBERS

Lever: A relatively simple and inexpensive arrangement. A lever actuates a piston inside a hydraulic reservoir. On some cars the lever itself is used to form a suspension member. Shock absorbers control wheel and spring movement.

Friction: The approved fitting for vintage sports cars whose springing was extremely hard. System depended on friction between dissimilar materials of the type used in brakes and clutches. Easy adjustment was an advantage.

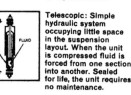
Telescopic: Simple hydraulic system occupying little space in the suspension layout. When the unit is compressed fluid is forced from one section into another. Sealed for life, the unit requires no maintenance.

Hydrolastic: An exclusive feature of B.M.C. front-wheel drive cars. The shock absorbing properties of the system are provided by rubber and water in combination. Compact, light and reliable, the system requires no maintenance.

Drawings from Castrol book CAR CARE

Corgi's model of the Formula 1 Grand Prix Cooper-Maserati (No. 156) shows the independent suspension in great detail. The V-12 cylinder engine is rear-mounted and the gearbox projects behind the final drive assembly.

CORGI MODEL CLUB NEWS

A MODEL CLUB MEMBERSHIP FORM WITH EVERY CORGI MODEL

SAMUELSON CAMERA VAN

(Right) Corgi's model (No. 479) of the Commer Camera Van in action. The camera and platform can be used on the roof or fixed to the front and rear of the van.

CINE-COMMER ON LOCATION: Television and newsreel camera teams are making increased use of light buses and vans when they film big public occasions. Sound camera, and all the equipment that goes with it, technicians and their belongings take up more room than can conveniently be carried in a car. In addition, the high roof of the van and the use of an extending platform, multiply the camera angles the team can use on every occasion. One of the most popular vehicles for this purpose is the 1-ton Commer. Some of Samuelson's Film Service fleet are illustrated in action here. This Commer is a specially adapted version of a 12-seater light bus with 1,725 c.c. under-seat petrol engine. The roof is strengthened to carry a camera platform and another platform can be attached to either front or rear at bumper level. The camera in use in our pictures is the popular Panavision equipment. In the action shot on the left, the Commer camera van and its crew are filming a recent visit of Billy Graham to London. Other close-ups show the versatility of the van.

35

CORGI MODEL CLUB NEWS

A MODEL CLUB MEMBERSHIP FORM WITH EVERY CORGI MODEL

THE MOTOR CAR—8
BRAKES & TYRES

More than 50 years of steady evolution have produced a modern car that is capable of impressive performance, comfort, and reliability. It is, of course, the responsibility of the owner to look after his car, and as far as safety is concerned the efficient work of both brakes and tyres is of paramount importance. Already the government have legislated for the efficient working of brakes on vehicles and soon further steps will be taken to ensure that all vehicles are fitted with roadworthy tyres.

Here in this story we describe two brake systems and two types of tyres most commonly associated with present day motor cars. At the bottom of the page we illustrate two Corgi models—the Buick Riviera (left) which has servo assisted drum brakes, and the Ferrari Berlinetta (right) which has discs all round.

BRAKES

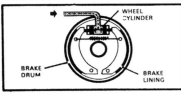
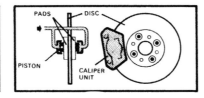

Drawings from Castrol book 'Car Care'

DRUM BRAKES

This type of brake is more than adequate for most family saloons. It works through expanding stationary 'shoes' against the inside of a revolving drum attached to the wheel. Even where disc brakes are used for the front wheels, drums are often used at the back because of the greater ease with which an efficient handbrake can be fitted.

DISC BRAKES

Disc brakes owe much of their present popularity to rapid development through motor sport. The principle is very simple—a disc spins round with the wheel and a fixed caliper squeezes it on both sides when the brake is applied. The number of caliper pads varies, and some discs have radial drillings to assist cooling.

TYRES

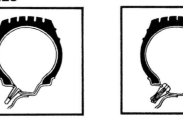

Cross section of tubed tyre. Valve is attached directly to tube.

Cross section of tubeless tyre. Valve is screwed to wheel itself.

Originally, wooden wheels with steel tyres were the only choice. Then came solid rubber tyres which were an improvement but were most cumbersome. The next development was the pneumatic rubber tyre, giving greater resistance to punctures, a smoother ride, longer wear, and better traction on both dry and wet road surfaces. The tubeless tyre is a comparatively recent invention; it gives less trouble, will hold its air for longer, and is less likely to deflate so suddenly when punctured. Some tyres have extra stiffening in the form of radial ply cording, whilst others have circumferential metal cording built in just beneath the tread. Such tyres give a slightly harder ride but the road-holding is much improved.

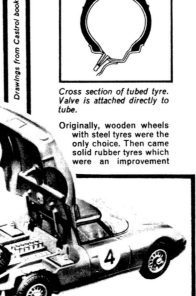

Corgi Model No. 245 Buick Riviera

Corgi Model No. 314 Ferrari Berlinetta 250 Le Mans

BIG BREAKTHROUGH BY CORGI

CORGI MODEL CLUB NEWS

A MODEL CLUB MEMBERSHIP FORM WITH EVERY CORGI MODEL

The built-in operating jacks and interchangeable wheels on the new Corgi model of the Mini-Marcos GT 850 represent a revolution in scale model car design. For normal 'motoring' the jacks are retracted into the chassis and do not interfere with the Corgi independent suspension feature, but when a wheel needs changing, each jack can be operated separately to raise the wheel from the ground, at the same time freeing the wheel which can then be removed. Should the car owner wish, all four jacks can be operated at the same time and all wheels removed.

Apart from this, the Corgi model of the Mini-Marcos incorporates a host of other features: wide opening doors, opening bonnet with detailed engine, well fashioned replicas of the Minilite magnesium alloy wheels as used in virtually all racing Minis, and another completely new feature: sliding front seats.

Long ago Corgi engineers realised that Corgi collectors and enthusiasts would dearly love to be able to change the wheels on their model cars. Tyres have been removable and replaceable since the earliest days of die-cast models. But, only now has a solution been found to the technical difficulties involved in providing removable wheels in a model under 3½ in. long, without complications or spoiling the realistic appearance.

Rugged, beautifully engineered and finished, the Corgi model still preserves the personality of the real vehicle. (Pictures right and left).

CORGI MODEL CLUB NEWS

A MODEL CLUB MEMBERSHIP FORM WITH EVERY CORGI MODEL

THE MOTOR CAR — 9
ELECTRICS

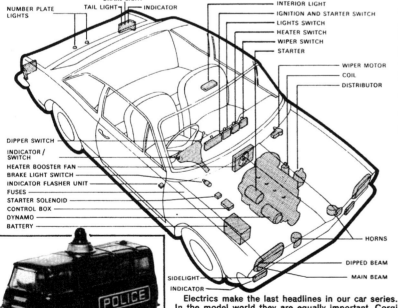

Drawings from Castrol book 'Car Care'

Electrics make the last headlines in our car series. In the model world they are equally important. Corgi engineers devised the battery-operated lighting system for the Commer Police Van (left) and the Cadillac 'Superior' ambulance. And have you seen the unique Trans-O-Lite lamps of the Rover 2000 and the Buick Riviera?

Corgi Model No. 464 Commer Police Van

 FUSES: There are few fuses in the modern car and it is best to consult the handbook for the location and amperage. It is wise to carry at least one spare especially when going on a long journey.

 HEADLAMPS: Most modern cars have 'sealed beam' headlamps. Failure could mean faulty wiring or a replacement unit. With older cars carry a spare bulb. Alignment of headlamps should be regularly checked and reflectors kept clean.

 SIDELAMPS: Vital for your own safety and that of other road users. And a legal requirement. They should be checked frequently to ensure that they are working properly. One or two spare bulbs are useful.

 STOP LAMPS: Rear lighting is just as important as head and side lights. Sometimes they can be damaged during reversing movements or the bulbs can fail. Make sure that both are working in your own garage before going out.

 INTERIOR LIGHT: Today known as courtesy lights because they are automatically switched on by a plunger as the doors are opened. Sometimes damaged as luggage is thrown on to the rear seats. The most common source of trouble is the bulb.

 WARNING LAMPS: Used increasingly in modern cars as a less expensive alternative to instruments. Occasionally unreliable, owing to bulb failure, but trouble in the light often indicates more serious trouble elsewhere. Watch oil and generator indicators.

 HORN: Less often in use in Britain than, for example, in Italy. Seldom known to fail, it should nevertheless be checked from time to time. Wiring can fray and brackets can shake loose.

 INSTRUMENTS: With the exception of the speedometer (another legal requirement) mileometer and oil pressure gauge, most of a car's instruments are electrically operated. When faulty, replacement is the best policy.

 WIPERS: The electric wiper is now universal. Attempting to wipe a dry screen is imposing an unfair load on motor and blades. The motor is fuse-protected. Blades, however, should be renewed annually.

 ACCESSORIES: When attaching electrical accessories, remember there are limits to the load you can impose on the system. But the alternator, now fitted to modern cars, will help to charge the battery quickly, even at low speeds.

CORGI MODEL CLUB NEWS
A MODEL CLUB MEMBERSHIP FORM WITH EVERY CORGI MODEL

COLOURFUL CARS

Over the past two years the fashion for decorating vehicles and cars has caused considerable comment. The famous 'Beatles' Rolls Royce was admired by many but also was the subject of great criticism from the 'purists'. Down Kings Road, the famous street in Chelsea, London, bangers and large American limousines can be seen painted all the colours of the rainbow. All round the country old taxis, minis, little Fiats, and Fords are seen carrying a full complement of foreign students with such slogans as 'Melbourne to London', 'New York to Moscow' 'South Africa to Hawai via Rome, Geneva, Frankfurt, London, Winnipeg and San Francisco!'

However, there are many other reasons for decorating vehicles not only for the pure fun of doing so. Military vehicles are specially painted for camouflage purposes in the same way as the Daktari Land Rover is painted to blend in with the jungle through which it travels. Racing cars are sometimes decorated with advertising slogans from the companies who act as sponsors. Stock cars in America and in Britain are plastered over with paint, numbers and slogans. It's a colourful world and, keeping abreast of the times, Corgi include many examples of these bizarre motor cars in their range.

John Lennon's chauffeur stands beside the 'flower' decorated Rolls Royce.

Racing cars taking part in the Indianapolis Grand Prix.

Stock cars spinning and turning at a British meeting.

The new 'Pop-Art' Mustang in the Corgi range.

Corgi 'Daktari' model of the Land Rover.

Corgi American Stingray stockcar.

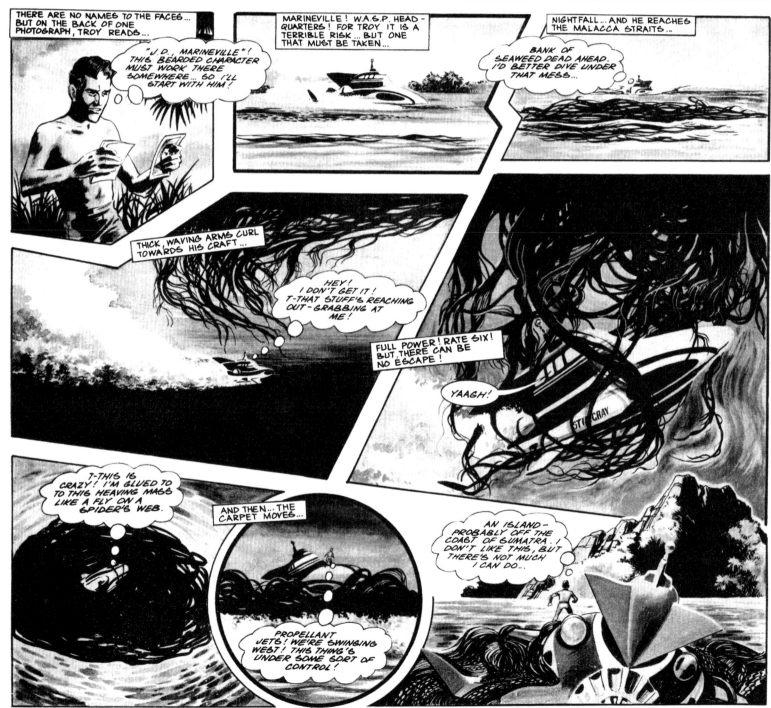

BUT TEMPEST KNOWS TOO MUCH...!

LET'S LOOK AT THE ROVER 2000 TC

Introduced in October 1963 after several years of development, the now famous Rover 2000 SC was immediately hailed by International Motor Writers as the 'Car of the Year'. This was following the success of the Rover B.R.M. Gas Turbine car which won awards at the famous Le Mans race by covering 2,592 miles at an average of 108 m.p.h. So popular was this Rover with the sporting and enthusiastic motorist that soon a twin carburettor version, the TC model, was produced developing 124 b.h.p. as against 99 b.h.p. from the single overhead camshaft 1978 c.c. engine, and propelling it to approximately 108 m.p.h. Coupled with extraordinary handling characteristics such as demonstrated here, equipped with rev counter, short gear lever connected to a 4-speed synchromesh gearbox, and all-disc brakes, this car became a firm favourite with racing and rally drivers. A main feature of the Rover 2000 is detachable body panels, bolted on instead of welded, and the main feature of the new exact and scaled replica Corgi model equipped with rally spare wheel is detachable wheels—not just tyres.

CORGI ROVER 2000 TC HAS DETACHABLE WHEELS!

With inbuilt separately operated Jacks, the wheels of the Corgi Rover 2000 TC can be lifted clear of the ground and, as all wheels are interchangeable, even the spare, it means quick pit stops can now be made.

NEXT WEEK: TEMPEST FORCED TO MAKE DEATH-LEAP!

RACING DRIVER Gerry Birrell

CORGI MODEL CLUB NEWS

A MODEL CLUB MEMBERSHIP FORM WITH EVERY CORGI MODEL

One young man fast making a name for himself in his native Scotland, and at motor racing circuits south of the border, is Gerry Birrell who lives in Glasgow. Gerry is only 23 and has followed his brother Graham's footsteps into racing. His early years in racing and rallying saw him very much the second string, but his employers Claud Hamilton Motors, who run Singer cars, saw Gerry's potential and last year he won every trophy there was to win in Scottish motor racing.

As a mechanic in his own right, he has painstakingly built up his own Singer Chamois for racing along with one of Scotland's leading racing mechanics Hugh Shannon from Perth. Shannon says of young Birrell: "He has a brilliant brain for someone so young and he is very kind on the car".

Last year, after finishing the highest placed Scot in the International Scottish Rally he was offered a drive with a leading private team in the Alpine Rally in France. As it turned out, the car couldn't start the event. Though he has competed in a number of rallies Gerry feels that he enjoys racing much more. This year he will again be out to hold on to his title of Scottish Saloon Car Champion and Scottish Speed Champion with his Singer Chamois.

He is also the factory driver for the Austro-Vee single seater racing cars based on Volkswagen parts and things are looking up.

Who knows, Gerry Birrell might well be another Jim Clark or Jackie Stewart? He doesn't like to think of himself in that class but outside observers have already noticed the stamp of genius in his driving. Time will tell.

The Singer Chamois driven by Gerry Birrell is a modified version of Rootes basic Imp engine—the Corgi model of which is extremely popular.

Corgi Model No 340: 1967 Monte Carlo Rally Sunbeam Imp

with rally details, opening rear window and a folding rear seat.

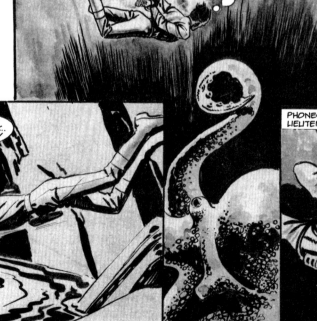

CORGI MODEL CLUB news F.A. CUP

A MODEL CLUB MEMBERSHIP FORM WITH EVERY CORGI MODEL

It was 96 years ago that the F.A. Cup Final was first held. In 1871 a handful of football clubs (15 in all) suggested playing a competition during the year for a cup which was to be called the Football Association Challenge Cup Competition. That year only twelve teams took part and the final was played at the Oval, Kennington, to a crowd of 2,000 spectators! As the years followed so more and more clubs joined the Association, the final being played at various grounds. It was not until 1922, when the British Empire Exhibition was being planned for Wembley that the present site for the stadium was built and the Cup Final found a home at last.

The F.A. cup itself has not survived without drama. On September 11th, 1895, the Cup was stolen from the shop window of a sports outfitters named William Shillcock in Newtown Row, Birmingham. A great hue and cry was set up and the harassed shopkeeper offered a special reward of £10 for the recovery—a princely sum in those days. But, it was never found.

Wembley vinyl playballs and sportsballs are made by the same company as Corgi toys. Many famous footballers have used Wembley balls for practice. Here we have Bobby Moore, O.B.E., the World Cup winning captain and captain of West Ham United with the Wembley World Champions ball and the Captain's Football.

Pictures: Top left the original cup; right: the replacement which will be handed to the 1967/68 winners. The old Cup winners' medal above (left) was replaced after World War II by the medal on the right.

MONACO GRAND PRIX

CORGI MODEL CLUB NEWS

A MODEL CLUB MEMBERSHIP FORM WITH EVERY CORGI MODEL

Once a year, in late May, the tiny fairytale principality of Monaco opens its borders to motor racing enthusiasts from all over the world. They stream into this South of France tourist and gambling resort to witness one of the most exciting and glamorous Grand Prix's on the World Championship calendar.

Tradition plays a large part in this Grand Prix and the whole town participates in the Motor Racing weekend mainly because the race itself is run on public roads throughout the town area. It is a truly wonderful sight as one views the race from one of the numerable road-side cafes, or from an hotel balcony, to see full-blooded Formula I single seater racing cars on full song hurtling through the narrow streets, clipping the curbs, and negotiating the tight corners and hairpin bends. The cars then scream along the waterfront on the fastest part of the circuit into the pitch black road tunnel, from which they emerge into the bright sunlight at over 140 m.p.h.

British cars have dominated the results over the last few years with wins by B.R.M., Lotus and Brabhams, but their age-old adversary Ferrari is always a force to be reckoned with on this circuit.

At present the lap record is held by a 2-litre Lotus-Climax 33 which was driven by Jim Clark in 2 mins 13.3 secs, at an average speed of 78.608 m.p.h. around the 1.959 mile circuit. This year the streets will echo to the sound of the V8, 3-litre engines in the Brabhams, Lotuses, Matras, and McLarens, and to the V12's of Ferrari B.R.M. Cooper, Eagle and Honda.

This is definitely a driver's circuit as the diagram shows, and all the Grand Prix racing cars in the Corgi range have over the last few years competed on this very gruelling road circuit.

Corgi Model No. 154 Ferrari

Corgi Model No. 155 Lotus-Climax

Corgi Model No. 156 Cooper-Maserati

CORGI MODEL CLUB news
A MODEL CLUB MEMBERSHIP FORM WITH EVERY CORGI MODEL

TRAILING A BOAT

Johnson V-6 runabout being towed by a Ford Cortina.

Modern glass reinforced plastic boats like the Glastron Sportsman are quite a bit lighter than the wooden equivalent of only a few years ago. The sophisticated family motor car of today, with its lively performance and good brakes, can tow a boat like this in perfect safety. Trailers too are of advanced design, often having independent suspension and hydraulic shock absorbers. With all this super equipment our Toronado driver could cruise with his boat on a motorway at speeds approaching as much as 100 m.p.h. In England, though, the law forbids anyone towing a trailer exceeding 40 m.p.h. This is just about the speed of a boat like the Glastron Sportsman; but on the water 40 m.p.h. feels more like 80—try it and see!

Launching a boat from a trailer is no great problem as the whole trailer can be pushed into the water and the boat simply

Frank Jutton—racing driver, boat-builder and Motor Boat & Yachting Class III champion.

floated off. At the end of the day the procedure is reversed: the boat being hauled back on to the trailer with the help of a winch fitted on the front end.

Boats like the Glastron Sportsman owe much of their development to racing drivers like Frank Jutton who is shown in our picture leaning triumphantly on his boat 'Merlin' in which he won the 'Motor Boat and Yachting' class III championships last year. Frank started his career racing home-made model boats and was a national champion for three years.

Class III races are held offshore around our coasts during the summer. If you want to watch one contact the Royal Yachting Association for a list of fixtures for the 1968 season.

Class III boats racing—this is the type of boat in which Frank Jutton became 1967 Champion.

Photographs by kind permission of MOTOR BOAT AND YACHTING.

Corgi Gift Set No. 36: Oldsmobile Toronado with trailer and the Glastron Sportsman V-171.

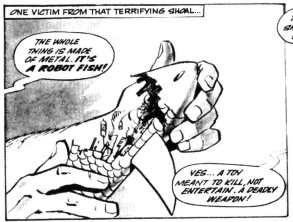

Last summer a party of eight from Friends' School, Lisburn, Northern Ireland, accompanied by a master, set out to deliver two Land-rovers to Afghanistan and India. Money had been raised by the school and friends to buy and deliver the Land-rovers as part of an Oxfam project for under-privileged countries. At the last moment it was discovered that the Land-rovers did not offer sufficient room for all the equipment and foodstuffs being taken. However, Pennyburn Engineering Limited of Londonderry came to the rescue by presenting the party with one of their special All Steel Tool Carrying Trailers—ideal for the job as the closed lids could be locked, proof against pilfering.

Leaving Belfast, the 'pilgrims' visited Oxfam H.Q.s in Oxford, spent a few days in London, then wended their way through France, Belgium, Holland, Germany, Austria, Yugoslavia, Bulgaria, Turkey, Iran and thence to Afghanistan. The journey to Kabul, capital of Afghanistan, was about five thousand miles and there the party left one of the Land-rovers with a team of eye-surgeons to help in their travelling clinics through this country, of whom about 60% of the population have eye trouble or are blind, though many could be cured with medical aid.

CORGI MODEL CLUB NEWS

A MODEL CLUB MEMBERSHIP FORM WITH EVERY CORGI MODEL

OVERLAND VENTURE '67

Some of the party unpacking the trailer en route in Yugoslavia.

The Land-rovers and trailer parked for the night in Turkey.

Resting up for a week, the master left with two boys to continue their journey to India where they delivered the other Land-rover and the Pennyburn trailer, to be used in an agricultural project.

This Oxfam project is doing excellent work in improving conditions for the people of this part of India and no doubt the Land-rover and trailer will be of immense value in improving the future of this and other similar projects and eventually raise the living standards of the people.

Two Corgi models—the Land-rover and the Pennyburn trailer.

PANDA CARS

CORGI MODEL CLUB news

A MODEL CLUB MEMBERSHIP FORM WITH EVERY CORGI MODEL

Out on patrol with the Coventry City Police.

NICK-NAMED THE 'Panda' because of its square dimensions and black and white colouring, the Police model of the Rootes Imp is gaining popularity around the country. Originally it was designed for patrol in Scotland around the lochs. For this exercise the police carried special equipment for dealing with all emergencies including rescue gear for those in difficulties on the loch.

Now, the use of this nippy little vehicle has spread to police forces in Devonshire and Coventry. Reproduced in the Corgi model are the police signs on the body of the car, the roof-mounted blue-beacon and, sitting at the wheel, a police driver in uniform. The rear window lifts and the back seat can be lowered.

Some of the equipment carried by the police in the 'Panda'.

Interior view of a Police Imp.

Corgi models of the 'Panda' Imp lined up outside a police station ready for action.

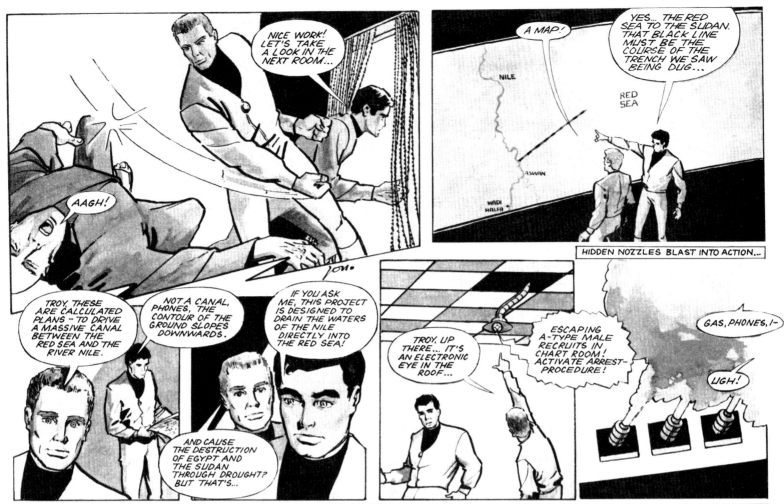

CORGI MODEL CLUB NEWS

A MODEL CLUB MEMBERSHIP FORM WITH EVERY CORGI MODEL

1: THE DRIVERS

The 1968 World Championship Formula One Motor racing series looks like being the closest and most exciting contest ever. This is a dangerous exacting sport only attracting brave men of the highest calibre.

We have listed 9 drivers who undoubtedly will be making a bid for one of the most challenging crowns of world sport. There are some we have not listed of the up and coming drivers, but on present indications it appears that the 1968 champion will be one of the drivers portrayed here.

There will be four articles covering Grand Prix racing, the drivers, cars, circuits, and finally a day in the life of the teams.

This is the first article covering the drivers and with three Championship races already contested, Graham Hill leads Denny Hulme by 14 points with a score of 24 points.

Corgi Grand Prix models include the Ferrari (top), the Cooper-Maserati (middle), and the Lotus-Climax (bottom).

Chris Amon: New Zealand. Ferrari No. 1. Won New Zealand Grand Prix, 4th World Championship 1967. Age 25.

Pedro Rodriguez: Mexico. B.R.M. No. 1. One of the most tenacious drivers on the circuit, winner of the 1967 African G.P.

Denis Hulme: New Zealand. McLaren-Ford 1967 World Champion, 2nd in contest so far for 1968.

Lodovico Scarfiotti: Italy. Cooper. Ex. Ferrari driver, drove Eagle 1967, changed to Cooper for 1968 races.

Graham Hill: England. Lotus. World Champion 1962. Leading 1968 Championship with two fine wins already.

Jack Brabham: Australia. Races cars of his own make. World Champion 1958, 1959, 1966, 42 years old.

Bruce McLaren: New Zealand. McLaren-Ford 1967 Can-Am Champion and Winner 1968 'Race of Champions' at Brands.

John Surtees: England. Honda. Ex World Champion Motor Cyclist, 1964 Formula One World Champion.

Jackie Stewart: Scotland. Matra-Ford. Ex B.R.M. No. 1. for 1968 driving the French Matra powered by a Ford V.8.

GRAND PRIX '68

CORGI MODEL CLUB NEWS

A MODEL CLUB MEMBERSHIP FORM WITH EVERY CORGI MODEL

2: THE CARS

Our story this week is on the Grand Prix racing cars that will be competing for the 1968 Championship.

In 1967 Denis Hulme the New Zealander became champion driving a Brabham. This year he has moved to McLaren and is partnering Bruce in the new McLaren M7A-Ford. Driving with Jack Brabham this year is Jochen Rindt, the young Austrian, and the car they will be driving has the new 3-litre V-8 Repco engine. BRM has a lighter chassis for their new V-12 engine, the car having been designed and built entirely at the BRM works at Bourne. Lotus have the same Cosworth-Ford 3-litre V-8 engine, but a new model is expected later in the year. Ferrari has a more compact new V-12 engine developing around 410 bhp and Cooper is using a new V-12 BRM engine.

Matra, designed and built in France, has a new V-12 engine, and from Honda a much modified 3-litre V-12 engine with a completely new cylinder head and valve gear lay-out is being used.

These then are the cars. Next week we will deal with the circuits.

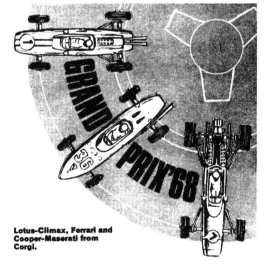

Lotus-Climax, Ferrari and Cooper-Maserati from Corgi.

BRM—V-12 engine.

Honda—V-12 engine.

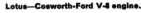

Lotus—Cosworth-Ford V-8 engine.

Brabham—V-8 Repco engine.

McLaren M7A-Ford—V-8 Cosworth Ford Engine

Cooper—V-12 BRM engine.

Matra

Ferrari—V-12 engine.

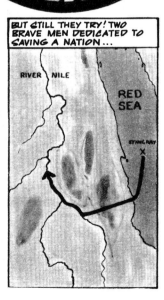

CORGI MODEL CLUB NEWS

A MODEL CLUB MEMBERSHIP FORM WITH EVERY CORGI MODEL

3: THE CIRCUITS — GRAND PRIX '68

With twelve countries promoting Grand Prix events qualifying for the 1968 World Championship Formula I races, the participants will be racing on a great variety of circuits around the world.

The location of these racing circuits take Grand Prix teams from one end of the world to the other. The circuits themselves pose an exacting challenge to the drivers as no two are alike—from the street circuit of Monte Carlo, to the gruelling flat out straights through the forests of Spa, and Nurburgring, to the buffeting banking of the Monza Autodrome, and on to the Mexico City, 7000 feet above sea level. It is a tremendous test of both modern day machinery and men. Corgi models include Ferrari, Lotus-Climax and Cooper Maserati Grand Prix cars, as illustrated in the artist's impression, top right.

S. African G.P.
Jan. 1st, Kyalami circuit 2.54m.
Winner: **J. Clark**.

Belgian G.P.
June 9th, Spa circuit 8.76m.
Winner: **B. McLaren**

British G.P.
July 20th, Brands Hatch circuit 2.65m.
Winner: ....

Canadian G.P.
Sept. 22nd, St. Jovite circuit 2.72m.
Winner: ....

Spanish G.P.
May 12th, Jarama circuit 2.1m.
Winner: **G. Hill**.

Monaco G.P.
May 26th, Monte Carlo circuit 1.95m.
Winner: **G. Hill**.

French G.P.
July 7th, Rouen circuit 4.09m.
Winner: ....

Italian G.P.
Sept. 8th, Monza circuit 3.57m.
Winner: ....

Mexican G.P.
Nov. 3rd, Mexico City circuit 3.07m.
Winner: ....

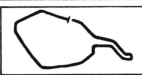

Dutch G.P.
June 23rd, Zandvoort circuit 2.6m.
Winner: ....

German (Euro) G.P.
Aug. 4th, Nurburgring circuit 14.2m.
Winner: ....

United States G.P.
Oct. 6th, Watkins Glen circuit 2.35m.
Winner: ....

CORGI MODEL CLUB NEWS

A MODEL CLUB MEMBERSHIP FORM WITH EVERY CORGI MODEL

GRAND PRIX '68

4 BEHIND THE SCENES

Excitement and glamour there is always, at watching the stars, and big names of motor racing, screeching round the tracks of the world at breakneck speeds. But, have you ever thought of the people, the teams, who make it all possible for driver and car to get on that track in time and in perfect order? We took the opportunity, at the recent Monaco Grand Prix, to watch and photograph two racing teams, Lotus and Cooper, at work during the practice sessions and the race. There is as much, or perhaps even more, excitement and tension in the pits during and after a race as on the circuit. Behind the scenes a dedicated bunch of men might work 48 hours on end without sleep, travel 2,000 miles in a lumbering transporter in a couple of days to get from one meeting to the other, and generally work extremely hard. These pictures illustrate some of the activities taking place: (A) Checking tyres, fuel, oil, etc. before practice laps start. When they are under way, times and laps are recorded, and any adjustments noted down. In the garage beforehand, gear ratios have been plotted out on graphs but it is very likely that when the car is run some changes to gearing are necessary. A close bond develops between the team chief, driver and mechanics, mainly because the driver's life depends to a large degree on the mechanics' skill. (B) After practice the car is taken back to the garage and, if no mechanical mishap has occurred, the car is checked over and made ready for the next practice, or the race itself. This may take most of the night and if, as in the case of an engine change, or if the driver has had a mishap damaging the car, it's all hands to work endeavouring to get it raceworthy. Here Colin Chapman is in conference with his crew. (C) It was Graham Hill's day at the 1968 Monaco Grand Prix when he crossed the line to win for the fourth time—a just reward for the mechanics and Lotus constructor, Colin Chapman. (D) After all the champagne has been consumed, and congratulations all round, it is back to work, loading up the cars and getting prepared for the next race only two weeks away.

Artist's impression of Corgi racing cars on the circuit: the Cooper-Maserati, the Lotus-Climax and the Ferrari.

CORGI MODEL CLUB NEWS

A MODEL CLUB MEMBERSHIP FORM WITH EVERY CORGI MODEL

BRITISH GRAND PRIX

Britain's premier motor racing event is without doubt the British Grand Prix, which is scheduled this year to be held at Brands Hatch on July 20th.

Many sterling contests have been held on the twisty, hilly, 2.65 mile circuit in Kent, but, on present form, this 1968 Grand Prix points to being a very decisive and critical race for many of the teams in the World Championship series.

'Brands' is a very exacting circuit where good car handling is a must because of the many humps and undulating surfaces which test a car's suspension to its maximum.

Already, the Ferrari team, with their No. 1 driver, Chris Amon, have done extensive testing around the club circuit, which incorporates part of the Grand Prix track, and many other teams are starting to set up suspensions and tyres in preparation for this race. Team Lotus have a good record in previous British Grands Prix, and must be favourites for this year's event but any driver who finished the race, and has the welcome sight of the chequered flag, will really have put in a tremendous effort in this, one of the world's toughest motor races. Illustrations show the start of a 'Brands' Grand Prix, and typical shots during the race, including a picture of the Corgi Lotus-Climax in a race scene.

CORGI MODEL CLUB NEWS

A MODEL CLUB MEMBERSHIP FORM WITH EVERY CORGI MODEL

BRITISH CAR TEST DAY AT MONZA

Italian enthusiasm for the fast car seems to be nothing less than a national characteristic. Nor is the interest confined to the Alfa-Romeos, Fiats and Lancias of their own country. Recently, the Society of Motor Manufacturers and Traders of Great Britain, which represents the car, truck and components production and marketing industry in the United Kingdom, invited members of the Italian motoring Press to try our cars on the famous Monza track, outside Milan. British cars which were lined up for inspection and test included Ford, Vauxhall, Standard-Triumph, Rover, Jaguar, M.G., Morris and Austin. Each was critically examined and expertly driven over several laps of this very fast circuit. All impressed the motoring writers who welcomed the opportunity of asking technical questions as well as handling the cars. Many Italian automobile journalists are just as familiar with the Corgi range as they are with British cars. They fully appreciate their beauty of line and finish and approve of the engineering that makes them best sellers all over the world.

(above) speeding round the circuit is the E-type Jaguar. Both driver and passenger wear crash helmets. (below) line up of British cars in the pits at Monza.

Here at the entrance to the circuit are traffic lights checking the cars safely on to the circuit. You will see the first car is an MGB, a very popular car as is also the Corgi model seen on the right.

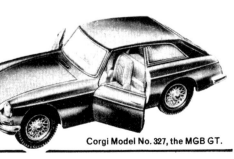

Corgi Model No. 327, the MGB GT.

CORGI MODEL CLUB NEWS

A MODEL CLUB MEMBERSHIP FORM WITH EVERY CORGI MODEL

OLDSMOBILE *Toronado*

Front view of the Oldsmobile Toronado is extremely impressive; (left) 'eyes' open for night-driving and shut (above)

Both the Corgi model and the real Oldsmobile Toronado are outstanding models. The real car because the engineers of the Oldsmobile division of General Motors in developing the front-wheel drive Toronado, produced the most unique American car in many years; and the Corgi model because it is one of the first miniature motor cars to have take-off wheels and individual jacks.

Styling of the Toronado is like that of no other car on the road today. Its floor is flat, allowing greatly increased interior dimensions and full six-passenger comfort in a coupe-bodied car. It is powered by a 6,965 c.c. V-8 engine mounted to the right of centre producing 385 b.h.p. at 4,800 r.p.m. The 15 in. wheel spiders are pierced with functional openings for air cooling of the cast brake drum fins. Other features of the Toronado include a draught-free ventilation system, which eliminates the need for quarter lights, power steering, vacuum-operated headlamp retractors inside rectangular headlamp housings which open up in seconds when the lights are turned on and retract automatically into the housing when the lights are turned off. A very impressive automobile.

Detail on the Corgi model is as impressive as on the real car, especially when one realises that the real car is 17 ft. 7 in. and the model is only 4½ in! Features include working retractable headlamps, take-off wheels and full interior trim.

(below) Latest Corgi model of the Toronado complete with 'Golden Jacks', interchangeable wheels and retractable headlamps.

Toronado from the rear showing the low lines of the coupe body.

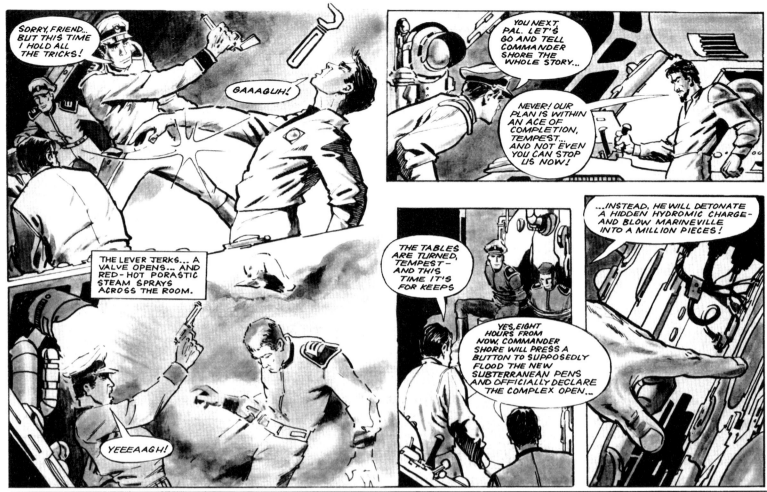

CORGI MODEL CLUB NEWS

A MODEL CLUB MEMBERSHIP FORM WITH EVERY CORGI MODEL

JAGUAR E-TYPE 2+2

There's always an admiring crowd in every town or village throughout the universe when it's parked. It's the dream car of all motoring enthusiasts, young and old. It's the E-Type Jaguar 2+2 coupe. Maximum speed 153 m.p.h., from its 4,235 c.c. 6-cylinder engine; long low profile. It's the world's Number One sports car.

Now, Corgi have made it possible for millions to own one. Though it be only 4¼ in. long, it still has, in miniature form, all the magic of its full size counterpart. Under the bonnet is a replica of the 4.2 litre engine; the doors open to reveal immaculate interior trim; the seatbacks tip, for access to the rear seat; and the rear door opens allowing the backrest for the rear seats to be pushed forward, for travellers with a lot of luggage to stow. The line and exterior finish of the model is in true Jaguar form, and particular attention has been paid to such refinements as plated wrap-round bumpers, air-vents on the bonnet and finely cast spoked wheels. It is this attention to detail, plus robustness, that has put Corgi Toys in the lead all over the world; for their engineers never forget they are making miniature cars with doors, and other moving features, that will be opened and closed as often as those of the real vehicle. The model must withstand the wear and tear of miniature motoring, in the same way as the real cars endure the hazards of the open road.

CORGI MODEL CLUB NEWS

A MODEL CLUB MEMBERSHIP FORM WITH EVERY CORGI MODEL

Most teenagers who are keen on cars and model making have attempted to translate their ideas of the perfect car on to paper. Some, good with their hands and equipped with the right materials, have gone so far as to build a detailed scale model of their dream-car.

Now, the 100,000-strong Vauxhall Craftsman's Guild, Kimpton Road, Luton, are sponsoring a £2,000 competition to encourage creative ability. Top prize is £500 and a trip to America. There is a £100 award for the best 'up to 15 year old'. Entry is open to United Kingdom residents up to the age of 20.

The new competition calls for the design and building of scale-model 'cars of the future'. Past competitions have produced very high standards of ingenuity and craftsmanship. Some of last year's 1,116 entries are grouped in the picture at the head of this article. On the extreme right, young entrants work on general arrangement drawings and scale problems, whilst on the left, a modeller smooths the finish of his entry. (Centre) Two creations by young stylists which may well be worthy of detailed study by the design department.

CAR DESIGNERS OF TOMORROW

Car of the future—today! Corgi's very advanced Batmobile with its trailer-boat.

CORGI MODEL CLUB NEWS

A MODEL CLUB MEMBERSHIP FORM WITH EVERY CORGI MODEL

Following in the footsteps of his chief, Enzo Ferrari, (who is a keen Mini-Cooper owner) Chris Amon the S.E.F.A.C. Ferrari No. 1 driver, flew into London just before the British Grand Prix to pick up his new 1275 c.c. Mini-Cooper 'S'.

Out of all the million or so minis built, this car has a specification of only four so far produced in the world. It was first tried out by that brilliant designer Alec Issigonis who had a 1275 c.c. Mini 'S' type Cooper and as an experiment he fitted it up with a Mini-Matic gearbox. Stirling Moss and Lofty England of Jaguar got on the band-wagon and had the 1275 'S' type modified to take the automatic transmission. Chris also made up his own specifications.

Take one Mini-Cooper 'S' 1275 c.c. and match it with an automatic transmission, plus a Downton Stage II tune, fit it out with rally seats and zoom! a 100 m.p.h. left-hand drive autostrada special.

Chris, who needs a car to commute between the international airport at Milan and the Ferrari factory at Modena, a distance of 120 kilometres, will no doubt surprise quite a few motorway racers when they try to keep the little green and white car in the rear vision mirror.

When he took delivery of the new Mini-Cooper, Chris was able to compare it with the Corgi replicas of the Rally Mini-Coopers and he was amazed at the exactness of the model cars and has now become an avid Corgi collector.

Chris Amon was as impressed with his Corgi Monte Carlo Mini as with his new 1275 c.c. Mini-Cooper 'S'.

TWO MINI-COOPERS FOR CHRIS AMON

Ferrari V-12 Formula I car on the track. 25-year-old Chris Amon is Ferrari's No. 1 driver.

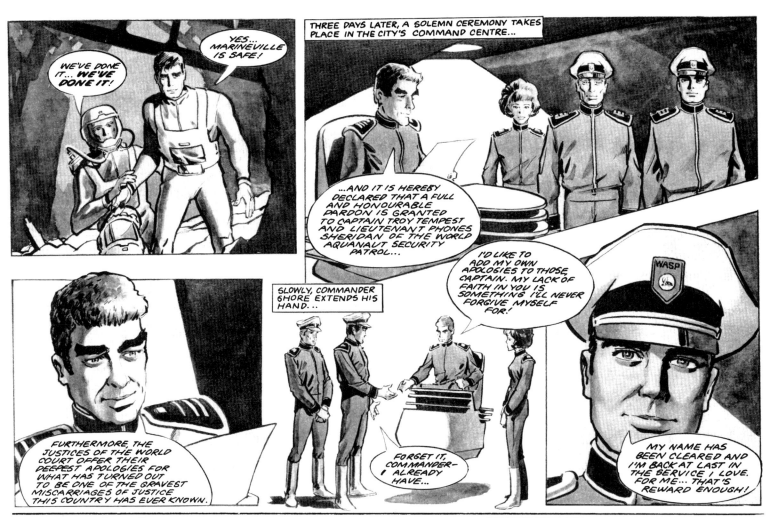

CORGI MODEL CLUB NEWS

A MODEL CLUB MEMBERSHIP FORM WITH EVERY CORGI MODEL

TOUR DE FRANCE

Inaugurated in 1903, the Tour de France is perhaps the most famous cycle event throughout the world. It embraces every type of road that France has to offer. Riders contend with the wooded hills of the Ardennes, the windswept Atlantic coast, the mountains of the Pyrenees, Massif Central and the Alps. It is the toughest race of its kind in the world, and its very toughness attracts world-wide radio, television and newsreel coverage. Throughout the whole of the three weeks of the race, the position of the leaders at each stage change with bewildering rapidity. Tactics play a vital role and mountain riders reserve their real effort for the Alpine sections, whilst the sprinters choose their moments on their own ground. The Tour is marathon riding at its finest. The winner for 1968 was the Dutchman Jan Janssen.

Illustrating this story are pictures of scenes taken on route. Bottom centre is a picture of the Corgi Tour de France Gift Set which includes a beautiful model of a Renault 16 complete with Paramount cine-camera and operator, as well as a typical competitor on a finely modelled racing cycle.

INTRODUCTION #2

STAND BY FOR ACTION!

++Priority Update from Commander Shore++

Attention all W.A.S.P. personnel, this is an urgent security update! Be sure to give this briefing your full attention as it concerns everyone stationed at Marineville and serving on W.A.S.P. vessels and installations across the globe.

Titan's latest hare-brained scheme is gathering momentum and it seems that nothing will stop him in his attempt to rally more undersea races to his alliance, causing chaos for the peoples of the land. Already we have seen his agents free prisoners from right under our noses, and lay waste to underwater cities who dare to oppose him.

His new allies include the powerful Astacus race who employ a devastating artificial tsunami cannon codenamed Tyrant Wave, the Altanteans who tried to mount a subterranean invasion of Marineville about a year ago, and the Harmonians with their hypnotic Deadly Concerto device. And those are only a few of the ones we know about – there have been whispers of other races joining the Titanican cause with each passing day.

Stingray's valiant efforts to thwart the growing Titanican menace have been fraught with peril. From routine patrols that ended in near calamity, to a close encounter with the Tyrant Wave weapon that left Stingray badly damaged and in need of major repairs. However, I want it noted for the record that Captain Troy Tempest and his crew have continued to perform their duties in the finest tradition of the service, even in the face of overwhelming adversity.

You may recall that one of Titan's cronies, an engineer called Scuplin, attempted to defect to the W.A.S.P. during the recent business with the Igneatheans. When he couldn't uphold his end of the bargain, we sent him back to Titanica in disgrace, figuring that Titan could deal with him. Instead, Sculpin managed to get himself back into Titan's good graces by creating an army of dolphin-piloted mechanical suits that were unleashed on Marineville, causing widespread disruption and damage.

Not content with devising his own technological terrors, Titan's audacious plan has also encompassed the theft of our latest attack submarine, Orca. In a gambit as daring as it was diabolical, Titan's surface agents managed to commandeer the vessel from Captain Dirk Dune and have taken it back to Titanica to add to their growing armada.

Orca is the most advanced vessel ever constructed by the W.A.S.P., outclassing all of our other undersea craft, including Stingray. Although he didn't knowingly aid in its capture, Captain Dune was subsequently drummed out of the W.A.S.P. for directly contributing to the ease by which Orca was stolen.

In light of this clear and present threat to the people of the world, I have instructed the crew of Stingray to seek out and recruit friendly undersea races to join the W.A.S.P. in repelling Titan's forces if they should attack Marineville. Whatever happens, he cannot be allowed to succeed in his plan – the consequences of such a victory are unthinkable.

All personnel standby for action – anything can happen in the next half hour!

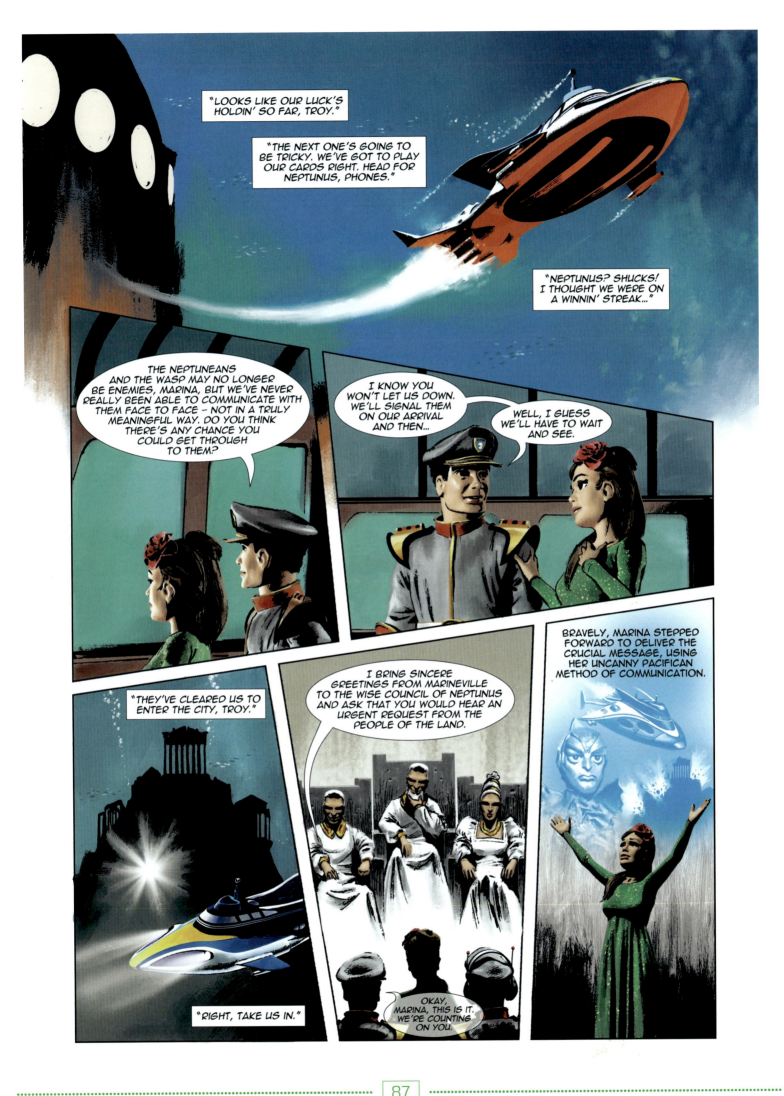

FEATURE
STINGRAY'S SPECIAL EXTRAS

The popularity of special seasonal editions of news stand comics wasn't lost on City Magazines and AP Films. Between 1965 and 1967, a variety of *TV Century 21* specials and extras were published. Chiefly released around summertime, seasonal specials were effectively bumper editions of regular news stand comics, often bridging the gap between the monthly *TV Century 21* and the equally popular line-up of annuals. They were similar in format to the regular comic but prioritised standalone stories, the type usually reserved for annuals. For the worlds of Gerry and Sylvia Anderson, these specials offered further expansive story material, enlarging the shared world of *TV Century 21*.

THE TV CENTURY 21 STINGRAY SPECIAL

Five of the seven *TV Century 21* specials/extras released during this time featured *Stingray* material, some with a greater emphasis on others. First out of the gate was the *TV Century 21 Stingray* Special released in May 1965. Despite being released towards the end of *Stingray*'s debut television run, its heavy focus on *Stingray* serves as an example of the super-sub's enduring popularity. The specials stuck to a mostly uniform line-up of comic strips,

(above) The cover of *TV Century 21* 1965 *Stingray* Special

text stories, breaking news pieces, in-universe and real-world features, along with the usual smattering of games and puzzles. The two text stories, *Barracuda 5* and *Ship of the Desert*, are illustrated with black-and-white stills. The photos in *Barracuda 5* are taken straight from the TV series itself, whilst those used in *Ship of the Desert* appear purposefully produced for this story, likely reusing sets and models from the TV episode *In Search of the Tajmanon* and the *Thunderbirds* episode *Pit of Peril*.

Barracuda 5 is one of the grimmest *Stingray* stories ever told; a bleakly thrilling revenge thriller in which *Stingray* races to stop W.A.S.P. lieutenant Tom Sands from piloting his Barracuda 5 W.A.S.P. submarine on a suicide mission to destroy Titanica to avenge the death of his brother, former aquanaut of the Barracuda 4 which Tom suspects Titan destroyed. *Ship of the Desert* is the more light-hearted of the two and features the return of the bombastic El Hudat and his clueless yet faithful aide Abu. We may safely assume that, of the two stories, *Ship of the Desert* at least was written by Alan Fennell himself, as it serves the entirely unusual role of being a sequel to a pair of TV episodes; *Star of the East* and *Eastern Eclipse*, both of which were written by Fennell. In *Ship of the Desert*, El Hudat and his brother are freed from jail following the events of *Eastern Eclipse*. However, the promise of freedom isn't enough for El Hudat and he succeeds in stealing Stingray in revenge against his imprisonment of the W.A.S.P.s.

The comic strips also featured in the 1965 *Stingray* special are rather lightweight in their storytelling compared to the darker storytelling which *TV Century 21* prioritised. They show Fennell apparently content to fall back on recycled elements from several of his own TV episodes, if he was indeed the author at work here.

In a quirk typical of British comics of this era, some stories are titled whilst others are left unnamed, as well as illustrated in a mixture of colour and black-and-white. *Double Trap* bears echoes of the TV episode *Trapped in the Depths* (another Fennell episode) with its premise of an underwater scientist using a doppelganger of Stingray to hijack the real one. This strip offers readers a delightful example of Ron Turner illustrating *Stingray*. Aside from his celebrated contributions to *TV Century 21*'s *The Daleks*,

Turner didn't illustrate much else in the comic but was a regular contributor to the seasonal specials and annuals. *The Big Freeze* retreads the basic premise of *Pink Ice* but is enlivened by some reliably stirring work from regular *Stingray* artist Ron Embleton.

Several months before the actual *Marina, Girl of the Sea* prequel strip would begin with the launch of the *Lady Penelope* comic in January 1966, the *Stingray Summer Special* presents us with Marina's debut comic adventure with an untitled *Marina, Girl of the Sea* story. This four-page adventure presents us with a curious continuity error. In this adventure, Marina succeeds in alerting the underwater city of Equapol of an oncoming invasion led by Titan but is then captured and enslaved by Titan for her actions. Stingray eventually crosses paths with Titanica with the strip's second half playing faithfully to the events of the first TV episode. The strip ends with Marina freed from Titan and becoming a welcome member of the Stingray crew.

This retelling of how Marina came to be a slave of Titan and eventual W.A.S.P. alumni is at odds with how the actual *Marina, Girl of the Sea* strip would come to explain these events. Not helping matters is the oddly lumpen, unappealing artwork, definitely at odds with the far superior efforts which Rab Hamilton would produce for *Marina, Girl of the Sea* strip once it launched in *Lady Penelope*. A trio of one-page comedy strips featuring Oink the Seal, illustrated by George Parlett, rounds things off for the *Stingray* Summer Special.

EXTRA, EXTRA!

1965 saw the release of two further *TV Century 21* seasonal specials. The *TV Century 21 Summer Extra*, released a few months after the *Stingray* one, prioritises much of *TV Century 21*'s Anderson-centric characters, with *Stingray* joined by *Fireball XL5*, *Lady Penelope* and *Agent 21*. *Stingray*'s untitled, four-page adventure sees

(above) The cover of *TV Century 21* International Special, 1965

Titan's Aquaphibians come close to destroying Stingray by secretly clamping a mine aboard Stingray's hull. Once again, Embleton enlivens a middling story.

The *TV Century 21* International Extra is one of the stronger publications, released as the title suggests in American, Canadian, Australian and New Zealand markets alongside the UK. *Stingray* is the priority at work here, boasting two comic strips and a text story compared to the single *Fireball XL5*, *Agent 21* and *Lady Penelope* stories. The first strip, an untitled five-page affair, emphasises the supernatural elements of Titan's underwater culture when the Stingray crew become entangled in a sacrificial ceremony when pursuing an armada of mechanical fish. The second comic sees Ron Turner in exhilarating form when the Stingray crew is tasked with rescuing the Delta Computer from having its vital research data destroyed by volcanic eruptions on the island of Mosoto before Marineville must bombard the island with hydromic missiles to quell its volcanic fury. Both comic strips feel much livelier than the preceding ones, embracing story material away from reliance on TV episodes, and feature a welcome involvement from Marina.

Alongside the robust comic strips, the short text story *Door of Danger* is a punchy affair involving Marineville suffering a devastating act of sabotage at the hands of Bereznik just as the W.A.S.P.s welcome an official visit from the World President, Nikita Bandranaik. *Door of Danger* is the only text story of *Stingray*'s to be illustrated by Embleton, and the inclusion of Bereznik and the World President is a welcome example of enhancing *Stingray*'s involvement in *TV Century 21*'s wider shared universe. Outside of quality story material, a double-page centre spread reveals how AP Films made *Stingray*, with lovely colour photos of Gerry and Sylvia Anderson, Reg Hill, John Read and further AP Films alumni engrossed in the production of the series. The accompanying images in particular appear to show scenes from *Tune of Danger* and *Set Sail for Adventure* being filmed, two episodes close together in production order.

Stingray's last substantial appearance comes in the *TV Century 21* Summer Extra. By now, *Thunderbirds* had blasted off in popularity, shifting *Stingray*'s status in *TV Century 21*. The super sub's solitary story inclusion comes in the Michael Strand illustrated *Tentacles of Terror*. With its four-page run-time, this adventure harks back to the earlier standalone *Stingray* comic stories, but is a spry, nimble monster affair and serves as a solid introduction to Strand's artistic take on *Stingray* before he'd take over as its main illustrator in *TV Century 21* itself later that year.

Beyond story material, a four-page spread provides readers with an in-depth examination of the Earth's various security defences, detailing the background of the World Government and Space Empire. Within this mini dossier of information, we learn how the World Aquanaut Security Patrol sits within the hierarchy of Earth's major security and military outfits, alongside the World Space Patrol, World Army/Air Force, World Navy, Universal Secret Service, Space Tracking Station, Security Council and Solar Council. It's an engrossing insight into the structure of *TV Century 21*'s shared world.

Stingray's very final presence in *TV Century 21*'s now dwindling line-up of seasonal specials comes in the form of a strikingly brief but still enjoyable *Marina* strip from the 1966 *Lady Penelope* Summer Special, the only time that the *Lady Penelope* comic itself would produce its own seasonal edition. This two-page adventure, illustrated by *Marina* regular Rab Hamilton, sees Marina come to the aid of a distraught underwater sea dragon whose offspring has vanished.

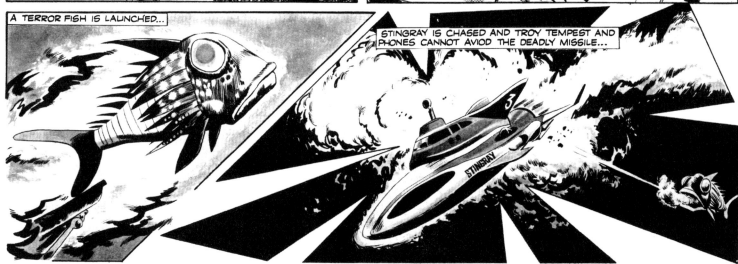

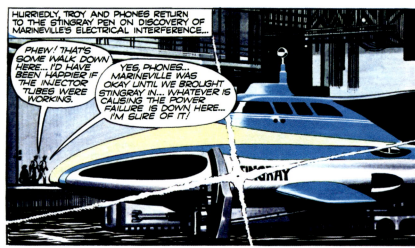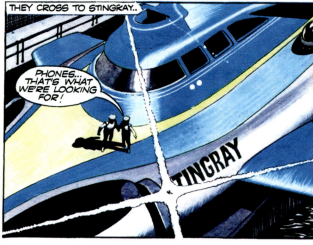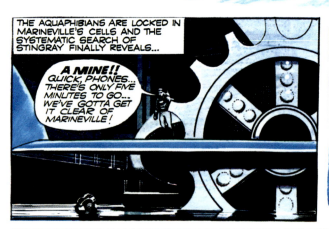

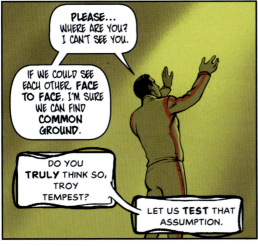

FEATURE

HOW THE MYSTERIOUS AND BEAUTIFUL MARINA MAY NEVER SPEAK AGAIN

Within a year of *TV Century 21*'s runaway success, AP Films' continuing experiences in the world of television tie-in publishing produced a plethora of accompanying publications including annuals, seasonal specials, novels, activity books, storybooks and other successful comics. This growing output of material would soon justify the establishment of AP Films' own separate publishing division to oversee this colossal operation. The girl-targeted *Lady Penelope* hit the newsstands in January 1966, and proved to be as large a hit as *TV Century 21*.

Compared to the mostly unified science fiction aesthetic of *TV Century 21*, *Lady Penelope* focused more on youthful swinging 1960s pop culture, with a balance of music, espionage and fashion content alongside numerous popular comic strips. The comic was edited by Gillian Allan, wife of *TV Century 21* script editor Angus Allan. An eclectic line-up of comics included strips based on *The Beverly Hillbillies*, *The Man from U.N.C.L.E.*, *Bewitched* and *The Monkees*, alongside original creations such as the spy-fi *Class Six Sterndof* and the comedic *What Did That Dog Say?*

Anderson characters naturally remained a regular staple in the comic. The *Lady Penelope* strip in *TV Century 21* may have drawn to a close, but her ladyship's self-titled comic magazine swiftly picked up where her previous comic adventures had left off. Where *TV Century 21* was now devoting its double-page centrespread to *Thunderbirds*, *Lady Penelope* matched this with its own centrespread dedicated to the International Rescue agent's continuing adventures, brilliantly drawn by Frank Langford with occasional contributions from Michael Strand and John Burns. On the back pages of *Lady Penelope*, another female Anderson character received similar attention.

(above) The cover of *Lady Penelope* comic issue #22, 1966

THE SILENT WORLD

Stingray's mute, underwater heroine Marina became the star of her own comic strip in *Lady Penelope. Marina, Girl of the Sea* ran for nine stories across Lady Penelope's first 88 issues. The initial six stories were illustrated by Rab Hamilton, whilst the remaining three were done by Colin Andrew. This strip follows the same format as *TV Century 21*'s preceding *Lady Penelope* strip – a prequel set before Marina becomes a member of the World Aquanaut Security Patrol. As such, it's more than likely that much of this strip was written by *TV Century 21* editor-in-chief Alan Fennell, who also authored *TV Century 21*'s earlier *Lady Penelope*, *Stingray* and *Fireball XL5* strips. Further standalone comic strip adventures for Marina would be included in the 1965 *TV Century 21 Stingray* Special and the 1966 *Lady Penelope* Summer Extra, as well as the *Lady Penelope* annuals from 1967 and 1968

Far removed from the hardware-heavy, male-dominated action of *TV Century 21, Marina, Girl of the Sea* drew readers into an enchanting world of underwater science fantasy, prising open avenues of *Stingray*'s world which the TV series didn't always have room to explore fully. Within this world, Marina lives in the city of Pacifica, a respected paradise of art, culture and higher thinking, along with her father Aphony who is the city's kind and peaceful ruler. The Pacificans live alongside many other underwater races and cultures in relative harmony. Knowledge of the existence of terrainean worlds appears non-existent, or at least not acknowledged throughout the strip. However, this tranquil existence remains under threat from the dangerous presence of the warlord Titan, who wishes to have all undersea races in his vice-like grip

In the sprawling, 23-part debut serial, occupying the first six months of the *Lady Penelope* comic, we see the full extent of Titan's villainous deceit against Pacifica, along with how Marina and her father come to have their voices robbed of them. Aphony seeks a peaceful end to Titan's terror by inviting him to sign an everlasting peace treaty between all underwater races within 10,000 marine miles of Pacifica. Titan initially accepts the invitation, but it's all a ruse to enable him to command an army of Terror Fish to destroy Pacifica. Injured and bewildered, Marina and Aphony, along with Pacifica's first minister Barinth, embark on a perilous mission to escape Titan's onslaught while convincing neighbouring races not to submit to Titan's rule, and that non-violent resilience is the only answer to his villainy.

After a string of deadly adventures, during which they gather remaining Pacifican refugees, many underwater races come together to help rebuild Pacifica, inspired by Marina and Aphony's messages of peace. This reconstruction naturally catches the attention of an enraged Titan. Demanding an audience with Aphony, Titan revisits the rebuilt Pacifica. Realising that destroying it a second time would be a futile gesture, and recognising Aphony and Marina's widespread influence, he murders Barinth and places a curse on the remaining pair, declaring that if either of them utters another word they would kill the other. Marina and Aphony may have rebuilt their paradise, but the pair become doomed to a world of silence.

This captivating story-arc starts the strip off in hugely spellbinding form. It's remarkable to think that something as lengthy and epic in scope as this was constructed to provide readers with a vastly more substantial and emotionally nuanced reason for Marina's muteness. A prime example of how the 1960s Anderson comics often took full advantage of traversing narrative territory which their TV counterparts avoided.

Adding to that captivation is Rab Hamilton's artwork. His elegant figurework and luxurious, suitably aquatic colours remain a consistent highlight throughout the *Marina* strip. Hamilton was also an artist of great economic precision in his detailing, which works to great effect within *Marina*'s one-page format. As well as the *Marina* strip, Hamilton's other most noteworthy output was his residential status as the primary artist on *TV Century 21*'s *Agent 21*, titled more precisely as *Special Agent 21* during its first two years. It later morphed into *Mr. Magnet* before shifting back to *Secret Agent 21* for the comic's final year. During *Agent 21*'s five-year run in *TV Century 21*, all but one of Brent Cleever's spy-fi adventures were illustrated by Hamilton.

Marina, Girl of the Sea is quite a different flavour compared to the brutalist, monochromatic spy-fi danger of *Agent 21*. Compared to other artists chiefly working on *TV Century 21*, Hamilton fares better in character likeness than technological hardware, although the *Marina* strip demanded little in that area. Hamilton's appealing line art can be attributed to his widespread contributions to girls' comics of the 1950s and 1960s, including serving on Fleetway's various romance titles and the two-year newspaper strip *I'm Patti* for the *Daily Mirror* between 1959 and 1961.

Despite being surely best known for *Agent 21*, Hamilton's *Stingray*-centric credits prove surprisingly extensive. As well as his prolific work on *Agent 21*, Hamilton was a regular contributor to the various Anderson seasonal specials, annuals and storybooks between 1965 and 1967. His other credits include the 1965 *Stingray* Television Storybook and the 1966 *Stingray* Annual, as well as the 1967 *TV Century 21*, the 1968 *Lady Penelope* Annual, the *TV Century 21* Summer Extra and *TV Century 21* International Extra from 1965, and the 1965 *Lady Penelope* Summer Extra.

After illustrating the *Marina* strip for its first 69 issues, Hamilton became the artist on *Lady Penelope*'s *The Girl from U.N.C.L.E.* strip, resulting in former *Eagle/Tiger/Lion* artist Colin Andrew stepping in. As the *Marina* strip neared its end, Andrew proved more than capable of continuing Marina's underwater adventures, but his character-likeness feels less confident than Hamilton's, whose presence is sorely missed.

FACING NEW DANGERS

After this debut serial, the strip focuses on Marina and Aphony's further adventures in maintaining as peaceful an existence as possible. In the second serial, the pair discover that they can still communicate with each other telepathically, addressing the communications barrier whilst the tragic curse remains in effect. Further serials see the pair (and Marina in particular) battling against more of Titan's schemes for underwater conquest whilst encountering similarly antagonistic forces and allying with other alien races. Semi-regular characters include the Prince of Oceanis and Staria, the niece of Titan. Aphony and Marina gain the upper hand still further when they discover that their telepathic abilities have the power to override Titan's Aquaphibians, a plot device that comes in useful several times during the strip.

The strip does much to portray Marina with a muscular sense of agency that she lacked in *Stingray*'s *TV Century 21* strip. Marina becomes reimagined as something of an anti-violent freedom fighter, regularly conveying messages of optimism against a backdrop of ever-present danger. Marina is consistently portrayed as an intelligent, brave, resourceful, sensitive and caring character. Aphony in turn often serves as a voice of reason to Marina's sometimes headstrong emotions. Storylines have a sharp focus on the struggle that Marina and her family and friends endure against Titan and other undersea aggressors, a constant battle between violent conquest and peaceful unity.

From issue #53 of *Lady Penelope*, *Marina, Girl of the Sea* shifted from being placed on the comic's back page to being situated within the comic itself, but now also reduced to being a black-and-white affair. The full-colour back page would now be occupied by a new ongoing strip that served as a prelude to the then-upcoming Gerry and Sylvia Anderson TV series *Captain Scarlet and the Mysterons*. This new strip would focus on a group of five female pilots who are brought together to undergo a series of strenuous missions to prove their worth to join a newly formed, top-secret organisation. These pilots would be given the codename The Angels…

As the *Marina* strip wears on, storylines become rather more light-hearted, suggesting that perhaps the strip was losing momentum in the wake of The Angels' arrival. One particular highlight from this twilight era sees Marina forced into marrying Prince Boldar, the obnoxious son of King Voltis, ruler of Caspia, only for Boldar to be injured by an underwater volcano, leaving Marina to decide if she should leave Boldar to die and avoid an unwanted life or to save him from further peril.

Marina's adventures come to an end, quite appropriately, with a retelling of *Stingray*'s first TV episode. These familiar events would now be retold from Marina's point of view, right down to the opening scenes of the World Security Patrol vessel Sea Probe attacked and destroyed by Titan's Terror Fish. The strip ends with Marina allying herself with the W.A.S.P.s, believing that, with the help of the terraineans, she may one day see Pacifica again and "smash the rule of the evil Titan forever!"

THE FULL STORY . . . HOW THE MYSTERIOUS AND BEAUTIFUL MARINA MAY NEVER SPEAK AGAIN!

Marina
GIRL OF THE SEA

Beneath the world's mighty oceans live many races of undersea people. Amongst the most respected is Aphony, ruler of the city known as Pacifica . . .

IN THE THRONE ROOM, APHONY TALKS TO HIS FIRST MINISTER...

BRING MY DAUGHTER MARINA TO ME, BARINTH...

AT ONCE, NOBLE APHONY.

THE BEAUTIFUL GIRL OF THE SEA IS HAPPY...

AH, MARINA... I WANT YOU TO PREPARE THE MOST LAVISH BANQUET PACIFICA HAS EVER SEEN. THERE WILL BE FOUR HUNDRED GUESTS...

HOW EXCITING... WHAT ARE WE TO CELEBRATE, FATHER?

BY TOMORROW EVENING I HOPE THAT ALL THE RACES WITHIN TEN THOUSAND MARINE MILES WILL HAVE SIGNED THE PLEDGE FOR EVERLASTING PEACE.

WHAT OF TITAN? HE IS OUR ARCH ENEMY... HE DOES NOT WANT PEACE.

BUT HE HAS AGREED TO COME... WE WILL HAVE TO TRUST HIM.

VERY WELL, FATHER... I WILL DO AS YOU WISH... BUT REMEMBER, TITAN IS EVIL!

YES... WITHOUT HIS SIGNATURE THE TREATY IS USELESS.

AS MARINA BECOMES INVOLVED IN THE PREPARATIONS FOR THE GREAT BANQUET, HER WORRIES LEAVE HER MIND...

WE WILL HAVE VINTAGE SEAWEED WINE, AND OCTOPUS SOUP...

WITH A MAIN COURSE OF ROAST ELECTRIC EELS AND SEAFOOD SALAD SERVED IN THE MOTHER OF PEARL SHELLS.

YES, AND THEN SEA ANEMONE COCKTAILS FOLLOWED BY OYSTER LIQUEURS.

THE BANQUETING HALL IS MADE READY...

NOTHING MUST GO WRONG. THIS COULD BE THE MOST IMPORTANT EVENING IN THE WHOLE OF OUR EXISTENCE.

LEAVE EVERYTHING TO US, YOUR HIGHNESS.

A MARINE DAY PASSES...AND THE GUESTS START TO ARRIVE...

THEN LATER, AFTER THE CONFERENCE HAS AGREED TO SIGN, A STRANGE VESSEL APPROACHES...

IT IS TITAN'S FLAGSHIP, BRINGING THE VICIOUS RULER OF TITANICA TO THE BANQUET...

MIGHTY TITAN... DO YOU PROPOSE TO SIGN THE TREATY?

WE SHALL SEE... BUT ONE THING IS CERTAIN... PEACE WILL COME TO APHONY TONIGHT— ONE WAY OR ANOTHER!

138

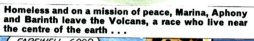

Marina
GIRL OF THE SEA

As Marina, Aphony and Barinth arrive on a peace mission at the city of Coonadas, they are fired upon. The blast throws Marina against a strange rock...

THE ROCK... IT IS THE DREADED GALAT...

THEN THERE IS NO HOPE... IT CONTAINS A DEADLY POISON.

FROM THE CITY OF SHIPWRECKS COONADANS SWIM OUT...

LOOK... IT IS APHONY THE PEACEMAKER.

WHAT HAVE WE DONE? OUR TEST FIRING HAS BEEN DISASTROUS.

THE COONADANS ARE ALLIES OF APHONY'S RACE. MARINA IS TAKEN INTO THE CITY.

GREAT APHONY... HOW CAN YOU FORGIVE US? WE BUILT THE WEAPON TO DEFEAT TITAN... INSTEAD WE HAVE CAUSED THE APPROACHING DEATH OF YOUR DAUGHTER.

I AM SAD, CALA. MARINA IS DYING AND MY HEART IS HEAVY WHEN I LEARN OF YOUR ATTEMPTS TO ATTACK TITAN. CEASE THIS USELESS PURSUIT.

USE THE MACHINE TO DEFEND YOUR CITY. TITAN WILL SOON TIRE OF WAR AGAINST AN UNWILLING RACE.

PERHAPS YOU ARE RIGHT, APHONY... YOU ARE WISER THAN I. BUT WHAT OF MARINA?

I CAN DO NOTHING... THE POISON IS BEYOND MY MEDICAL KNOWLEDGE.

THERE IS ONE CURE... AN ANTIDOTE... IT HAS BEEN PERFECTED BY TITAN'S SCIENTISTS...

BUT IT REMAINS UNDER STRONG GUARD IN THE SEDAC LABORATORY.

I KNOW OF THE PLACE, APHONY. IT LIES TWENTY MARINE MILES FROM TITANICA.

LEAD MY WARRIORS TO THE BUILDING, BARINTH. THEY WILL GET THE MEDICINE.

SELECTING THREE COONADANS, THE FAITHFUL BARINTH LEAVES...

IF BARINTH IS DELAYED BY ONE MARINE MINUTE, IT WILL BE TOO LATE TO SAVE MARINA.

MAKING ALL HASTE, BARINTH REACHES THE SEDAC LABORATORY...

THE AQUAPHIBIANS ARE HEAVILY ARMED... AND THEIR WEAPONS ARE SUPERIOR TO OURS.

YES... BUT WE MUST SWIFTLY FIND A WAY INTO THE BUILDING... OR MARINA WILL DIE!

149

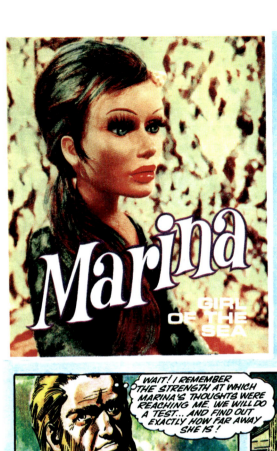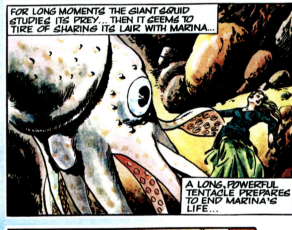

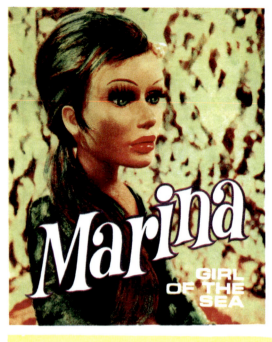

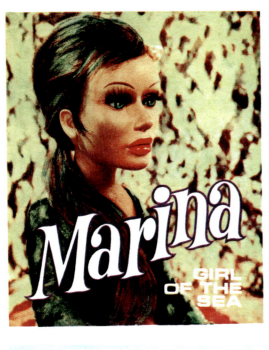

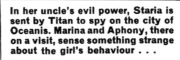

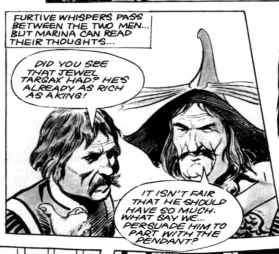

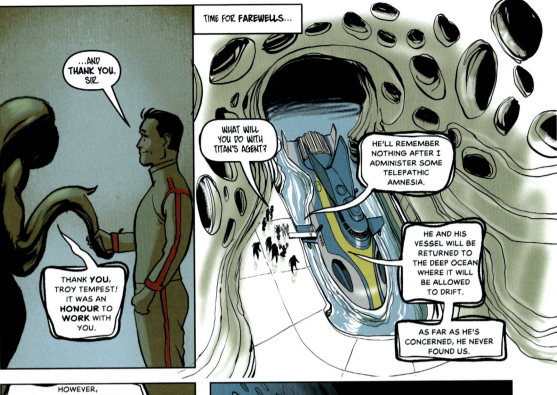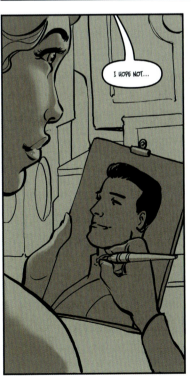

FEATURE
COUNTDOWN TO STINGRAY

In February of 1971, following the demise of TV21 in September 1969 and its lacklustre merger with *Joe 90: Top Secret* to become *TV21 & Joe 90* (which would last until September 1971), a new comic appeared to reignite the creative and commercial momentum of *TV21*. Polystyle Publications head honcho Arthur Thorne tasked Dennis Hooper and Century 21 Publishing book editor Roger Perry with spearheading a new space-age comic that suited the mood of the times, the glossy result being *Countdown*. With its mixture of fresh adventures for older and current Anderson properties, i.e. *UFO*, and real-world articles covering then-current Apollo Moon missions, *Countdown* felt like quite a deliberate stab at creating *TV21* 2.0.

Hooper brought a combined familiarity with Anderson content and a key knowledge of comics production, having

(above) The cover of *Countdown* issue #1, from February 1971

served with *TV Century 21* as art editor from beginning to end. Compared to *TV Century 21*'s structure of a constant flow of multi-part serials, Anderson properties in *Countdown* took a more unusual approach. *UFO* remained a solid fixture between 1971 and 1973, but the older Anderson characters flirted between a mixture of multi-issue arcs and standalone adventures, often appearing at an unpredictable schedule within the comic's pages. Don Harley became *Thunderbirds*' resident artist for its renewed string of adventures in *Countdown*, but the likes of *Captain Scarlet and the Mysterons*, *Zero X*, *Fireball XL5* and *Stingray* were illustrated by a wide variety of artists.

With the former *TV Century 21* art editor at the

helm, editor-in-chief Hooper inevitably looked to *TV Century 21* for inspiration to produce a suitable follow-up; perhaps for a fresh audience of readers who were hooked on *UFO* and may have been catching any one of the *Supermarionation*-era productions in repeats. *Stingray* enjoyed an intermittent presence throughout *Countdown*'s early months between March and July. Amongst its five stories are a pair of serials and three standalone affairs. Like many of the other Anderson strips in *Countdown*, the *Stingray* strip was illustrated by a revolving line-up of artists, with some familiar talent returning from *TV21*.

Countdown ran on a far more skeletal staff than *TV21*. Hooper claimed writing the *Doctor Who* strip as well as *Countdown*'s self-titled space opera epic, which utilised the spaceship design from *2001: A Space Odyssey*. He's also credited with writing *Countdown*'s *Thunderbirds* and *Fireball XL5* strips, so it makes sense to think he would have handled the remaining Anderson strips too.

MODEL MISSIONS

Stingray's handful of stories in *Countdown* are a mostly solid bunch, with enjoyable premises and competently illustrated, even if the vibrant colours of *TV21* are sorely missed. Story-wise, there's little here that feels out of place within the world of *Stingray*, perhaps serving as further evidence of Hooper's authorship of the strip. Story topics start off strong, ranging from environmental disasters to cyber espionage and arctic terror, before reaching the strip's undeniable highlight with *The Waters of Hyde*, a bizarre adventure involving Stingray journeying to Mars and discovering a race of underground cave dwellers

Stingray's *Countdown* era starts off in muscular form with the natural underwater disaster of *Terror of Titan*. Its meaty premise sees Stingray grapple with the two-pronged threat of a rampaging series of underwater earthquakes causing colossal tidal waves, which in turn become exploited by Titan for his own nefarious ends.

The Cyber Saboteurs certainly benefits from being a serial rather than a standalone adventure. Compared to the straight-faced environmental catastrophe of *Terror of Titan*, *The Cyber Saboteurs* feels much wilder as a story. During the story's events, the duplicitous Professor Morrison succeeds in framing Troy for the destruction of a robot tanker, which has quite definite echoes of *TV21*'s *Marineville Traitor* storyline.

The Cyber Saboteurs balances its surreal threats with entertaining action and unexpected moments of humour through the witty dialogue, and the doppelganger saboteurs under Morrison's control have more than a hint of Mysteron agents in both purpose and function. Speaking of comparisons, however, Phones even refers to the saboteurs as Cybermen. Rather on the nose for a comic which carried a major *Doctor Who* strip! Phones himself is the break-out star of the strip, becoming its protagonist halfway through the story's events.

Returning *TV Century 21* alumni Michael Strand illustrates this opening pair of stories. Whilst it's pleasing to see his figurework remaining mostly consistent throughout these pages, his action sequences aren't as enthusiastic as they could be. His best work certainly remains within *TV Century 21*.

Polar Peril from *Countdown* #13 stands as perhaps the dark horse of *Stingray*'s *Countdown* era. This downbeat, moralistic tale of humankind's unconsidered plundering of natural resources coming into conflict with the world of an underwater species picks up where the environmental leanings of *Terror of Titan* left off. Strong hallmarks of *Stingray* TV episodes can be found, with the unintended disturbance of another species recalling *Sea of Oil*, along with the clash between the W.A.S.P.s and the trigger-happy Captain Hail of the World Navy echoing the events of *The Man from the Navy*. The inclusion of the World Navy itself, along with appearances from the World Security Council, shows a storyline operating with confidence in *Stingray*'s source material.

Artist Colin Page crafts a moody atmosphere with the Antarctic setting, and whilst his brush techniques come off as rather aggressive compared to other *Stingray* comic artists, they inject a welcome vigour into the action sequences. His character likeness is less successful – Atlanta is drawn with wildly different hairstyles by each artist!

STRANGE WATERS

The surreal highlight of *Stingray* in *Countdown* comes in the epic *The Waters of Hyde*. This seven-part story occurs between issues #15 and #21 and is the only *Stingray* story in *Countdown* to be illustrated by multiple artists. Michael Strand produces the artwork for issues #15 and #17, but Rab Hamilton illustrates the majority of the story.

Stingray is tasked with venturing to Mars when a survey team investigating a newly discovered subterranean ocean on the red planet goes missing. Troy and Phones soon discover a seemingly welcoming alien race that exists within the heart of Mars, but when exposed to the race's underground waters Troy and Phones undergo a hideous transformation into uncontrollable ape-men. *The Waters of Hyde* mercilessly zigzags in tone between sci-fi mystery and boisterous monster horror, and climaxes in a finale so oddly extreme that it had to be adjusted when the storyline was reprinted in Polystyle's 1983 Stingray Special. This special also reprinted *Terror of Titan*, *Polar Peril* and *Deep Sea Doom*.

Deep Sea Doom holds the unusual stature of being the last ever original *Stingray* comic story of the 20th century. This final original outing for *Stingray* in *Countdown* is illustrated by Brian Lewis, who also worked on *Countdown*'s *Fireball XL5*, *Captain Scarlet* and *UFO* strips. Lewis's artwork is undeniably the weakest of the *Countdown* era artists working on *Stingray*. His depictions of Stingray itself are decent enough, but his ragged line art makes his take on the characters something of an eyesore.

Deep Sea Doom also takes advantage in clarifying what exactly the number 3 on Stingray's rear fin denotes. Several explanations have been offered by other *Stingray* media, including the number 3 meaning that Stingray launches from pen 3 within Marineville, or that the current Stingray is in fact Stingray Mark III. By comparison, *Deep Sea Doom* embraces the idea that Stingray is in fact the third vessel amongst a much larger core fleet of submarines of the World Aquanaut Security Patrol, and that other submarines of the same design co-exist similar to the Fireball fleet of the World Space Patrol.

Deep Sea Doom thrusts Phones back into the spotlight when a mysterious villain from his younger days returns seeking revenge against himself and other aquanauts. One by one, the crews of W.A.S.P. vessels are being killed and their submarines destroyed, with Spearfish and Barracuda successfully targeted. Further vessels Thornback and Moray are briefly seen during the story's events, along with the Spearfish bearing the number 4 on its fin, implying that W.A.S.P. has (or at least had!) five such submarine craft to its name.

Following *Deep Sea Doom* in issue #22, *Stingray* maintained a continual presence in *Countdown* via reprints of earlier stories from *TV21*. Issue #23 began with The *Ghosts of Station Seventeen*, initially with its opening instalment in full glossy colour before the rest of the story was reprinted in black-and-white. This odd trend of some instalments sticking in their original colour format but mostly reverting to black-and-white would remain. Following *Ghosts* came reprints of *Aquatraz*, *The Uranium Plant Invasion*, *The Weather Mystery*, *The Monster Weed* and *Junk Jeopardy*.

By the time *Junk Jeopardy* began, *Countdown* had morphed into *TV Action + Countdown*. The last instalment of *Junk Jeopardy* in issue #71 in June 1972, marked the end of a seven-year run for *Stingray* being a semi-regular presence in British news stand comics. It would be another 20 years before *Stingray* would blast into comic book action once again, this time under its own title.

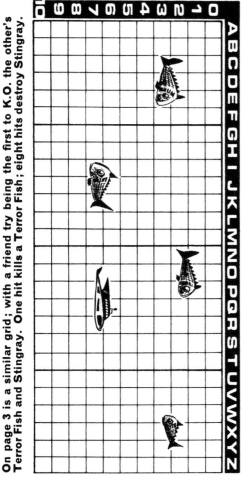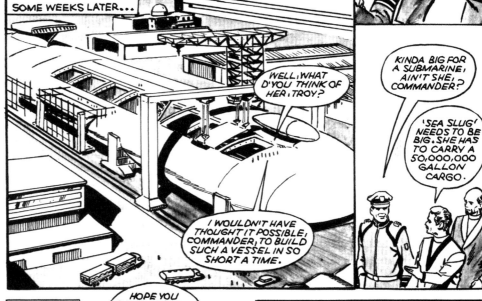

SEEK and DESTROY!

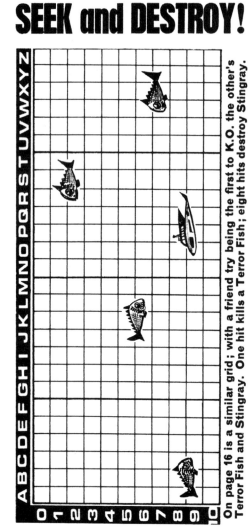

On page 16 is a similar grid; with a friend try being the first to K.O. the other's Terror Fish and Stingray. One hit kills a Terror Fish; eight hits destroy Stingray.

RIGHT ON TIME...
EVERYTHING IS READY. NOW, JUST SET THE SIGHTS ON THESE UNSUSPECTING FOOLS...

TWO STUNNING SHOCK RAYS SHOOT FROM THE CAR'S HEADLIGHTS...
"PERFECT! TWO DIRECT HITS!"

The Quatrodecimalopede
That's right, a bicycle-built-for-fourteen. Jeff Kilburn—that's him on the far left—and 13 of his friends put together this 30-foot-long bicycle in his back garden in Coundon, Warwicks. And only three months work, too. You can imagine the difficulties in turning corners on a two-wheeled machine weighing one and a half tons fully loaded.

ONCE AGAIN PROFESSOR MORRISON'S CAR SPEEDS TOWARDS THE REEF...
"I'D BETTER GO BACK AND COLLECT PHONES SHERIDAN WHILE YOU'RE TREATING THESE TWO."
VERY WELL. WE WILL FINALISE THE PLANS FOR MARINEVILLE'S DESTRUCTION WHEN YOU RETURN.

MEANWHILE, AT MARINEVILLE...
"WHAT THE...?"
"WHERE'S THE COMEDIAN WHO TRIED TO DENT MY SKULL..."

SECONDS LATER PHONES REPORTS TO COMMANDER SHORE...
"I THINK IT'S ABOUT TIME WE INVESTIGATED PROFESSOR WESLEY MORRISON."
"CAN I HAVE PERMISSION TO SCOUT CRAGSTONE REEF, SIR? I HAVE A FEELING WE'LL FIND A FEW ANSWERS DOWN THERE."
"P.W.O.R., COMMANDER."

BEFORE LONG, STINGRAY SHOOTS FROM THE OCEAN DOOR...
"REMEMBER YOU'RE ON A RECONNAISSANCE TRIP, PHONES. DON'T TAKE ANY ACTION WITHOUT ORDERS."
"SOMEHOW I THINK I'LL FIND THE KEY TO TROY'S INNOCENCE OUT THERE."

"WHY CRAGSTONE REEF, PHONES?"
"THE WEED CAUGHT ON MORRISON'S CAR IS PECULIAR TO THAT AREA, COMMANDER."

AS STINGRAY APPROACHES THE REEF...
"WASP VESSEL APPROACHING... IT'S STINGRAY!"
"IT COULD BE JUST CO-INCIDENCE. LET THE BATTLEFISH DEAL WITH IT!"

STRANGE SIGNALS ARE SENT TO DEEP OCEAN AND...
"I'VE NEVER SEEN ANYTHING LIKE THEM. GIANT BATTLEFISH! AND THEY'RE GOING TO ATTACK."

Continued next week!

Men among the moon rocks

In the rocky region of the Fra Mauro highlands, the Apollo 14 astronauts had to thread their way between large boulders in an attempt to climb the 400-foot summit of Cone Crater. They fell short of the top by only 50 feet. This picture shows Alan Shepard standing in front of a moon boulder. Dust clings to his boots and the legs of his spacesuit.

STINGRAY

The Waters of Hyde

While exploring the underwater sea discovered on Mars, Troy and Phones are trapped in Stingray between two artificial cliffs. The sea between the cliffs is pumped away leaving Stingray resting on the sea bed. Suddenly friendly Mertians appear and invite the two Wasps to their city. After a feast, which ends with a swim...

"IT'S HAPPENING TO US... OUR ONLY HOPE..."

● ART: MICHAEL STRAND © 1971 Century 21 M. Ltd.

AS THE TRANSFORMATION IS COMPLETED, PHONES JOINS THE CROWD, WHILE TROY REALISES HE HAS LOST THE POWER OF SPEECH.

"PHONES... WE'VE GOT TO FIGHT IT... GET BACK TO STINGRAY... I'M NOT GETTING THROUGH..."

FIGHTING THE URGE TO JOIN WITH THE OTHERS, TROY FORCES HIMSELF TO LEAVE...

"MUST KEEP THINKING OF STINGRAY... NEED HELP TO SAVE US..."

SUDDENLY THE SPELL OF TRANSFORMATION ENDS...

"COME... THERE IS ONE WHO WOULD BETRAY US... HE MUST BE STOPPED!"

"KEEP GOING... NEARLY THERE..."

"FASTER... HE MUST NOT REACH HIS REFUGE..."

"WE HAVE HIM..."

"NOT YET..."

"YOU SHALL NOT WIN..."

"IT'S LOCKED..."

"BACK TO THE CLIFF... WE WILL LET THE WATERS DO THEIR WORK..."

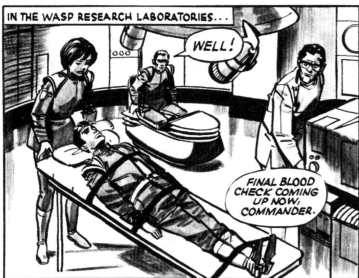

FEATURE
THE FLEETWAY YEARS

Several of Gerry and Sylvia Anderson's Supermarionation productions enjoyed a colossal revival in popularity in the early 1990s. *Thunderbirds*, *Stingray* and *Captain Scarlet and the Mysterons* all received early evening broadcasts on BBC Two, and once again proved to be a huge success in both viewer numbers and merchandise tie-ins. While these three series all received prime-time viewing slots, *Joe 90* was rather unceremoniously shunted into an early Saturday morning slot on BBC One, and therefore failed to find a comparable level of success.

An onslaught of merchandise accompanied these reruns, among them a variety of series-specific comic books published by Fleetway Editions Ltd. For the first time ever, *Stingray*, *Thunderbirds* and *Captain Scarlet* each received their own dedicated comics specifically for them (as did *Joe 90*). These 1990s comics were a mixture of reprints of classic *TV21* serials and newly produced material, including new storylines, episode adaptations, vehicle cutaways, character portraits and more, all packaged to evoke the newspaper attitude of *TV21*, but with a more modern design aesthetic.

Alan Fennell returned to edit these comics, having spent his post-*TV21* career in other avenues of the publishing industry. He brought with him several returning artists, including John Cooper and Malcolm Stokes, as well as managing to coax Mike Noble out of semi-retirement to provide a handful of portraits and covers. *Thunderbirds the Comic* was the obvious winner, running for a staggering 66 issues between October 1991 and May 1994. The revival of public interest in *Thunderbirds* both on television and the news stands quickly prompted the return of *Stingray* which was first broadcast on the BBC between

(above) The cover of *Stingray the Comic* issue #1, from October 1992

September 1992 and December 1993. Inheriting the Friday evening slot from *Thunderbirds*, the series was rerun in a haphazard fashion, taking numerous breaks during its run before settling into a Sunday lunchtime slot near the end of its initial BBC screening.

Whilst not quite hitting the peaks that *Thunderbirds* had enjoyed, *Stingray*'s 1990s return was still a huge success for the then 30-year-old series. In terms of comics published, *Stingray the Comic* was the second longest-running of the 1990s Anderson comics, running for 32 issues across two volumes between October 1993 and May 1994. Both the *Thunderbirds* and *Stingray* comics would begin their runs balancing classic *TV21* and *Lady Penelope* storylines with newly illustrated adaptations of classic TV episodes. Not entirely by coincidence, these would be adaptations of episodes originally written by Fennell himself.

Whilst *Thunderbirds the Comic* would go on to prioritise new comic storylines, including the hugely ambitious prequel epic The Complete *Thunderbirds* Story, *Stingray the Comic* struggled to produce new material beyond episode adaptations. Nevertheless, these adaptations are lively, succinct and faithful interpretations of several of *Stingray*'s early episodes. The adaptations begin with a two-part summary of *Stingray*'s debut episode, published in issues #4 and #5. It's more of a prose summary, but with superb illustrations by *Stingray* superfan Steve Kyte. Full comic strip adaptations of TV episodes began in earnest from issue #5 with a three-part adaptation of *Plant of Doom*. This was followed by *Hostages of the Deep*, *The Big Gun* and *The Ghost Ship*. John Cooper would illustrate *Plant of Doom*, *Hostages of the Deep* and *The Big Gun*, whilst Nigel Parkinson of *The Beano* and *The Dandy* would illustrate *The Ghost Ship*.

(above) Art by John Cooper from *TV21 & Joe 90* issue #20, February 1970

Cooper was a regular contributor to various Anderson annuals of the 1960s and 1970s, including *Thunderbirds*, *Joe 90 Top Secret*, *TV Century 21* and *Countdown*. He also illustrated a pair of *Captain Scarlet* storylines in *TV21* during its final months and served as the main artist on the *Thunderbirds* strip in *TV21 & Joe 90* between September 1969 and June 1970. His work on the *Stingray* episode adaptations is a pleasing late-career highlight, with an emphasis on well-tuned character likeness and vibrant colours. Parkinson's brief contributions to these 1990s Anderson comics offer a more caricatured take on the *Stingray* characters compared to Cooper's efforts, while his take on *The Ghost Ship* even opens with a colourfully dramatic depiction of the destruction of the jet liner Arcadia, an event mentioned but not seen in the TV episode itself.

These adaptations were chiefly scripted by Graeme Bassett, co-author of the 1993 *Captain Scarlet* series guidebook with Chris Drake, and a regular contributor to Anderson fanzines of the 1980s. Bassett also wrote the ongoing Undersea Races Fact Files, a series of ongoing dossier-style reports of Stingray's various underwater enemies and allies. These text features greatly elaborated on the mostly unspoken backstories of these one-off characters, with Bassett often tying them into the wider shared world originally seen in *TV21*. Issue #23 of *Stingray the Comic* for instance featured a backstory on Klorata and Fragil, the villains from the TV episode *Deep Heat* (although Klorata was named Torata on screen). The fact file describes how following on from the events of the TV episode, the last two survivors of Centralius had apologised for their actions and are lending invaluable assistance to Captain Paul Metcalf and Captain Brad Holden, joint leaders of a combined W.A.S.P.-World Army/Air Force mission against the Atlantians – and two names that should be familiar to fans of *Captain Scarlet*...

From issue #17, *Stingray the Comic* would fall back almost entirely on archive material, perhaps as a result of both *Thunderbirds* continuing to be the standout hit of Anderson titles for Fleetway and the then-forthcoming arrival of *Captain Scarlet*, which featured original comic storylines right from the off. *Stingray*'s lengthy run in *TV Century 21* surely helped in justifying the comic's main focus on classic material. After 24 issues published on a fortnightly basis, *Stingray the Comic* would morph into *Stingray Monthly* from October 1993. This format would last for eight issues until all of Fleetway's Anderson comics were brought under one publication. The *New Thunderbirds Comic Featuring Captain Scarlet and Stingray* ran on a fortnightly basis from May 1994 until March 1995.

Having utilised the vast majority of *Stingray* serials from *TV Century 21* and even standalone stories from *TV Century 21*'s specials/extras throughout *Stingray the Comic* and *Stingray Monthly*, the super-sub became an increasingly scarce presence in *The New Thunderbirds*. New story material was still being produced for *Thunderbirds* and there remained plenty of quality archive material from *TV Century 21*'s *Captain Scarlet*, *Zero X* and *Fireball XL5* strips, as well as Anderson strips from the *Lady Penelope* comic. *Stingray* would stay afloat through reprints of standalone comic stories from the 1960s annuals, but these couldn't help but look garish alongside the more sophisticated artwork from the *TV Century 21* comic itself. *Stingray*'s presence in *The New Thunderbirds* would come to something of a weary end with a reappearance of the *Plant of Doom* adaptation between issues #78 and #80, a rather transparent admittance of the well running dry for story material.

Even with the BBC Two revivals coming and going, plus dwindling sales of *The New Thunderbirds*, enthusiasm remained. *The New Thunderbirds* finally ceased publication in May 1995, but undeterred by this apparent end of the road Fennell debuted a fresh self-financed publication hot on its heels. *Thunderbirds Are Go!* ran for a miserly eight issues, focusing almost exclusively on archival reprints to a rapidly dwindling readership. *Stingray* gained a last throw of the dice by Fennell's raiding of the vaults once more and utilising the *Countdown*-era stories. *Thunderbirds Are Go!* ended publication just as the comic was about to conclude its reprint of the bizarre *The Waters of Hyde* storyline, leaving its final instalment tantalisingly unpublished.

Stingray's various appearances in 1990s comics remain one of the more modest success stories of Anderson TV tie-in comics, but in a time before reprints of classic material became commonplace, the *Stingray* comics' mixture of new and classic material offered something for fans young and old.

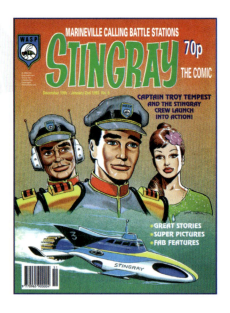

(right) The covers of *Stingray the Comic* issues #6, #10 and #15 from December 1992, February and April 1993.

(opposite) The original cover artwork of *Stingray the Comic* issue #9 from February 1993, courtesy of the artist © Andrew Skilleter

Starts Today: "Hostages of the Deep" - Part 1

295

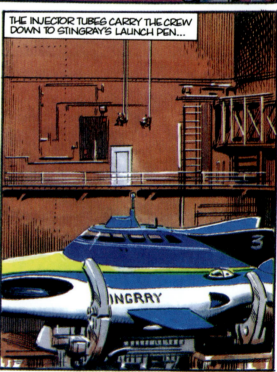

Starts Today: "Hostages of the Deep" - Final instalment

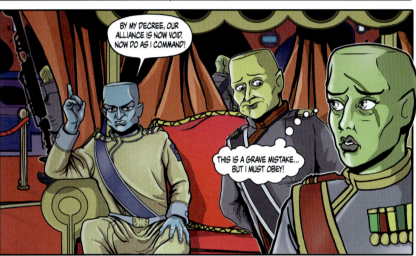

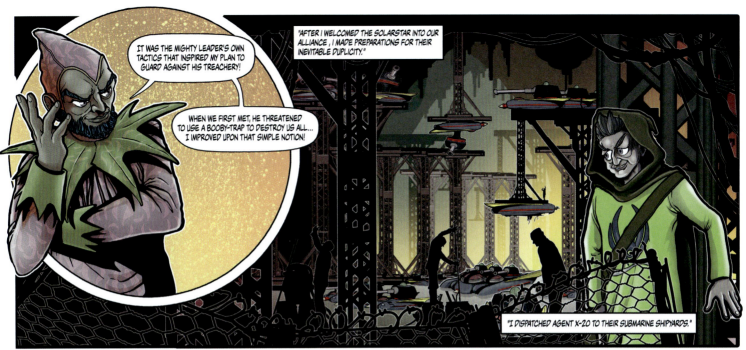

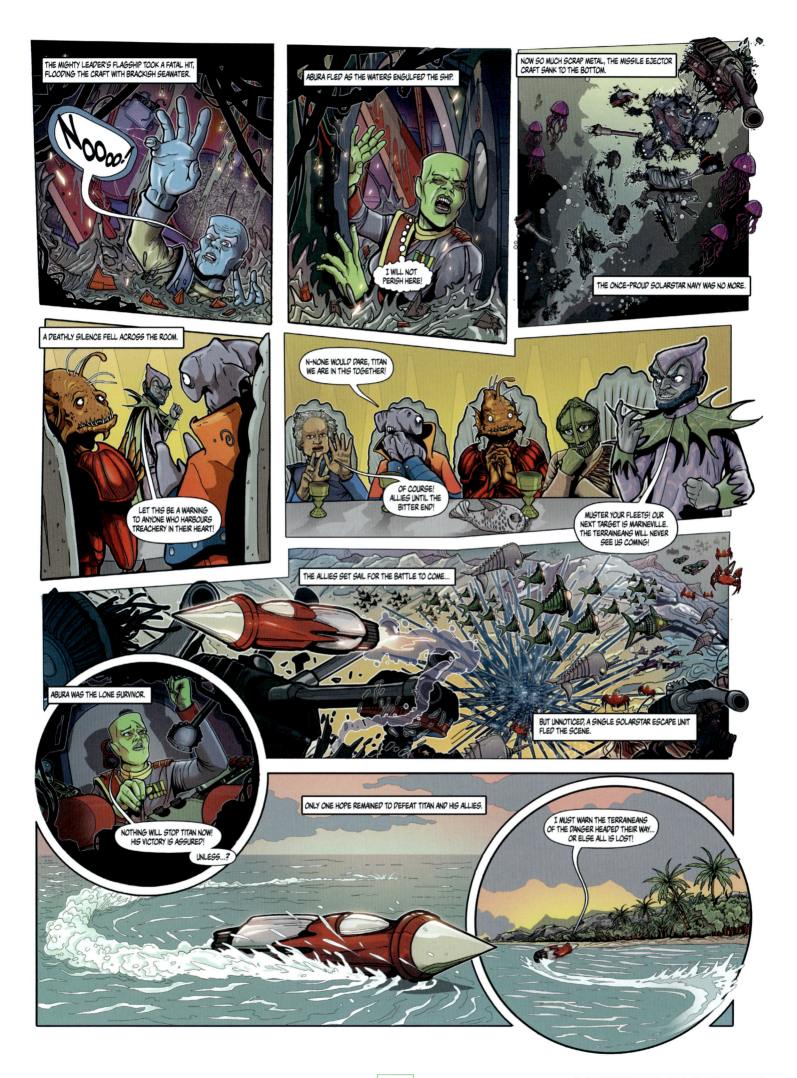

Starts Today: "The Big Gun"

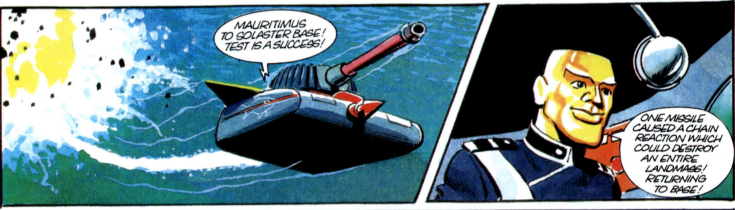

"The Big Gun" - Part 2

313

"The Big Gun" - The Conclusion.

"The Ghost Ship" - Part 2.

FEATURE
STINGRAY'S FUN DAYS

Alongside Fleetway's popular line-up of Anderson comics throughout the early 1990s, readers could enjoy additional comic spin-offs in other publications. *Thunderbirds*, *Stingray* and *Joe 90* all had ongoing strips in *The Funday Times*, the long-running children's comic supplement featured in *The Sunday Times*, which were published to accompany each of their respective comics.

These strips offer an intriguing insight into just how popular Anderson shows were throughout the 1990s, with these classic properties appearing alongside comic strips of *Spider-Man* and *Asterix*. A *Captain Scarlet and the Mysterons* strip appeared in the pages of *News of the World*'s *Sunday* magazine, alongside ongoing strips for *Mighty Morphin Power Rangers*, *Sonic the Hedgehog* and *The Flintstones*. *The Sunday Times* strips occupied one page

(above) The masthead of *The Funday Times* for the duration of the *Stingray* strip

per instalment, whereas the *Captain Scarlet* strip and its Sunday magazine companions were fashioned in a more traditional newspaper strip style, with just three panels per episode.

Unsurprisingly, *Thunderbirds* had the lengthiest run in *The Funday Times*, running seven multipart adventures between issues #110 and #246. Several of these were later recycled into the 1993 *Thunderbirds* annual and even *The New Thunderbirds* comic once all other pre-existing comic material had been exhausted. In between *Thunderbirds*' run in *The Funday Times*, a *Stingray* strip ran for a pair of storylines between issues #158 and #185 to tie into the release of *Stingray the Comic*.

Both the *Thunderbirds* and *Stingray* strips in *The Funday Times* were illustrated by Keith Page, one of Alan Fennell's most frequent artistic collaborators during this time. Page also illustrated many of the episode adaptations and original storylines in Fleetway's *Thunderbirds* comics. John Cooper illustrated *Joe 90*'s *The Funday Times* strip as well as *Sunday*'s *Captain Scarlet* strip.

At first glance, the two *Stingray* storylines from *The Funday Times* mark the nearest the super-sub would ever come to having brand new comic book adventures produced during the 1990s, but close inspection of

330

their story material proves otherwise. The first untitled storyline is a rather transparent welding of the basic threats from the TV episodes *The Master Plan* and *Secret of the Giant Oyster*, a pair of episodes written by Fennell himself. This storyline sees Titan unleash a strange chemical weapon against Stingray which attracts fierce underwater creatures. The second is an expanded rendition of the standalone strip *Night Raid* from the 1965 *Stingray* annual, in which the Stingray crew battle against an invasion of gargantuan mechanical crab mechas from Titanica.

Both storylines may be admittedly lightweight in their plots, but Page's colourful art and enthusiastic panel composition keep the proceedings entertainingly lively. His depiction of Stingray during aquatic battle scenes can't help but make one wish that there had been further original comic stories for the series during this time.

The first storyline would be reprinted in the 1994 *Stingray* annual, but curiously enough, they wouldn't be recalled to action in the same way that the *Thunderbirds* strips were in helping to bulk out *The New Thunderbirds* in its twilight years. Ultimately, they remain fun, visually upbeat outings which undoubtedly helped to bolster *Stingray*'s profile in the 1990s.

(above) The cover of *The Funday Times* issue #158, from September 1993

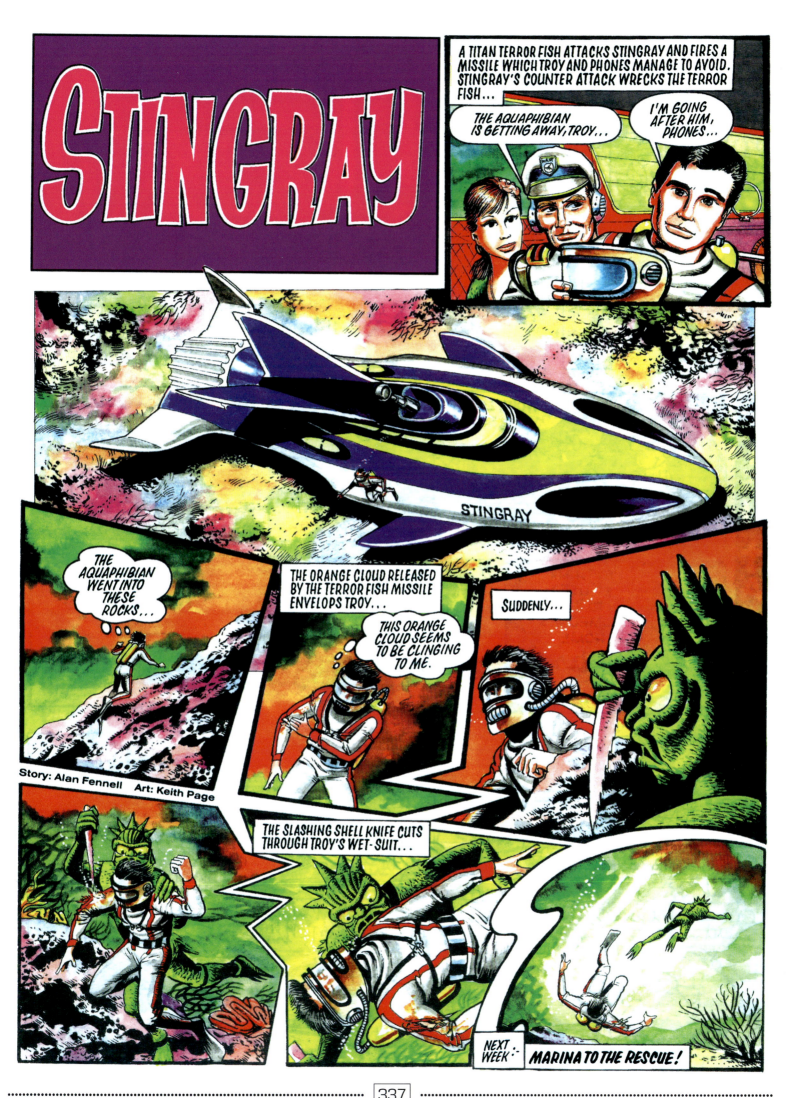

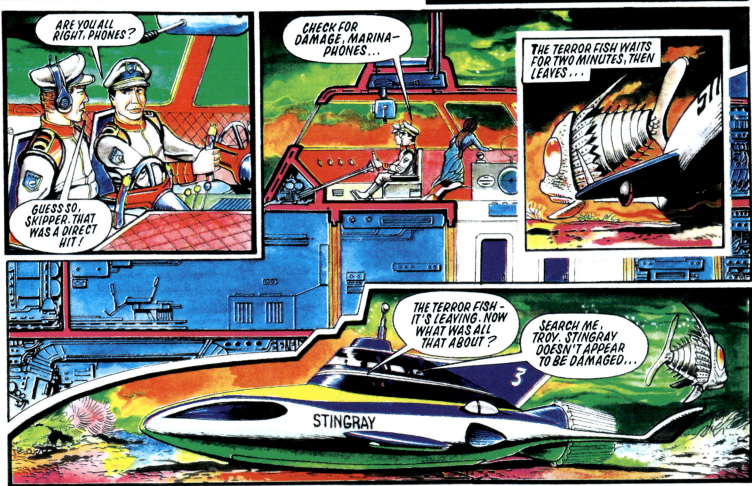

Story: Alan Fennell Art: Keith Page

STINGRAY

STINGRAY HAS BEEN OUT OF COMMISSION WHILE TROY, PHONES AND MARINA DEAL WITH A STRANGE ORANGE CLOUD THAT ATTRACTS UNDERSEA CREATURES. TITAN HAS USED THE TIME TO SEND A FLEET OF TERROR FISH TO ATTACK MARINEVILLE...

THERE ARE TOO MANY OF THEM FOR US, PHONES. BACK OFF. WE'LL HAVE TO CONTACT MARINEVILLE FOR ORDERS.

IN ITS UNDERGROUND EMPLACEMENT, MARINEVILLE IS SO FAR SAFE FROM TITAN'S MISSILES...

STINGRAY TO TOWER. WE'RE NOT FAR FROM THE OCEAN DOOR...

Script by Alan Fennell   Art: Keith Page

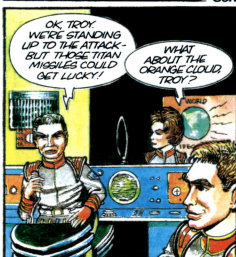

OK, TROY. WE'RE STANDING UP TO THE ATTACK - BUT THOSE TITAN MISSILES COULD GET LUCKY!

WHAT ABOUT THE ORANGE CLOUD, TROY?

WE'VE MANAGED TO SHAKE THE FISH OFF FOR THE MOMENT, ATLANTA, BUT WE CAN'T STAND STILL FOR TOO LONG - THEY'LL BE BACK!

A COUPLE OF WASP SUB-CRUISERS ARE APPROACHING THE AREA NOW, TROY. YOU LEAD THEM IN.

P.W.O.R. COMMANDER!

MINUTES LATER, THE SUBMARINE CRUISERS MAKE CONTACT WITH STINGRAY...

THE BATTLE FORMATION IS READY...

STINGRAY TO SUB-CRUISERS 1 AND 2 - LET'S GET RID OF THOSE TERROR FISH! FULL SPEED AHEAD!

NEXT WEEK: THE CONCLUSION!

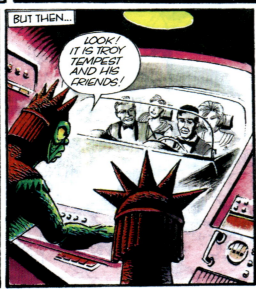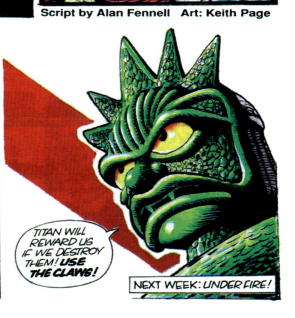

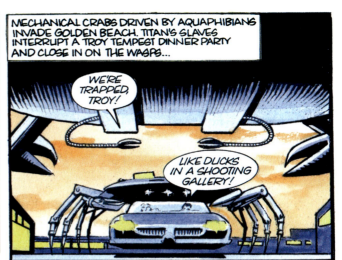

Script by Alan Fennell   Art: Keith Page

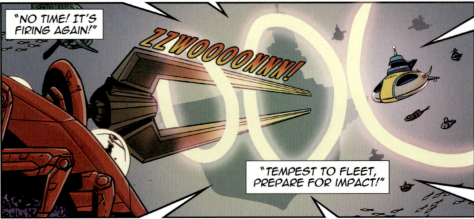

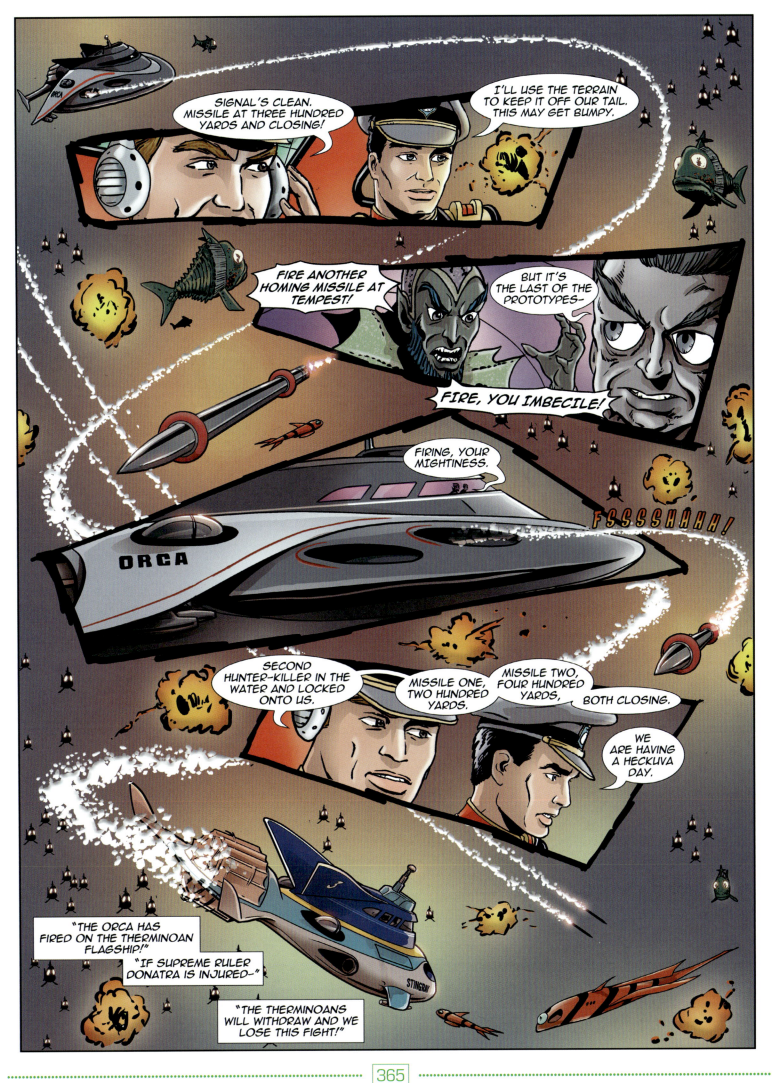

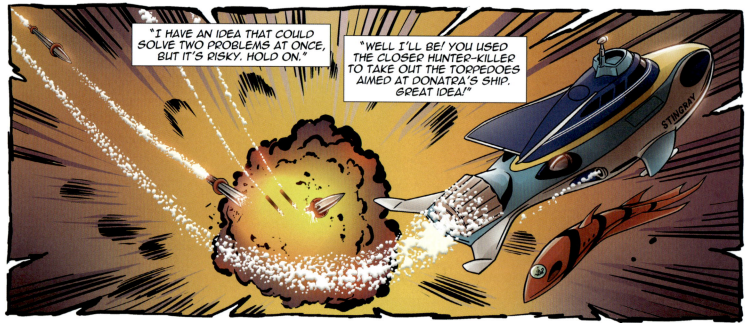

MEANWHILE... "TITAN'S ARMADA IS WHAT WE EXPECTED..."

"...BUT WHERE ARE HIS GROUND FORCES?"
MAYBE THEY WERE DESTROYED BY THE SOLARSTARS WHEN THEY TURNED ON HIM?
OUR LUCK'S NOT RUNNING THAT GOOD.
GREAT NEPTUNE!

WHAT, MAN? SPEAK!
TITAN'S GROUND FORCES ARE *ALREADY* ON THE SURFACE!
RANGE, ONE POINT FIVE MILES AND HEADING OUR WAY.
HOW CAN THAT BE?

"THE ATLANTEAN NARWHAL SHIP DRILLED THROUGH THE GROUND AND CAME STRAIGHT UP THOUGH THE UNDERSEA CLIFFS."
"THEY HAD TO STAY AWAY FROM THE SEISMIC SENSORS UNDER THE BASE."

"THEY'RE HEADING FOR THE AIRFIELD – GOING AFTER OUR STRIKE FIGHTERS!"
"NOW WE HAVE A CHANCE. FIRE INTERCEPTORS!"

"DIRECT HITS! TWO THIRDS OF THEIR STRIKE FORCE HAS BEEN DESTROYED!"

SEISMIC ACTIVITY ALERT! ANOTHER VESSEL APPROACHING THE EMPLACEMENT!
SOUND GENERAL QUARTERS!

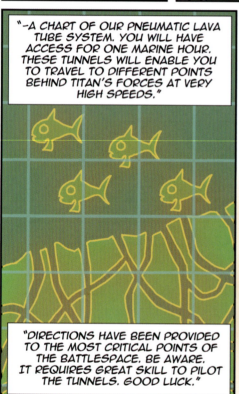

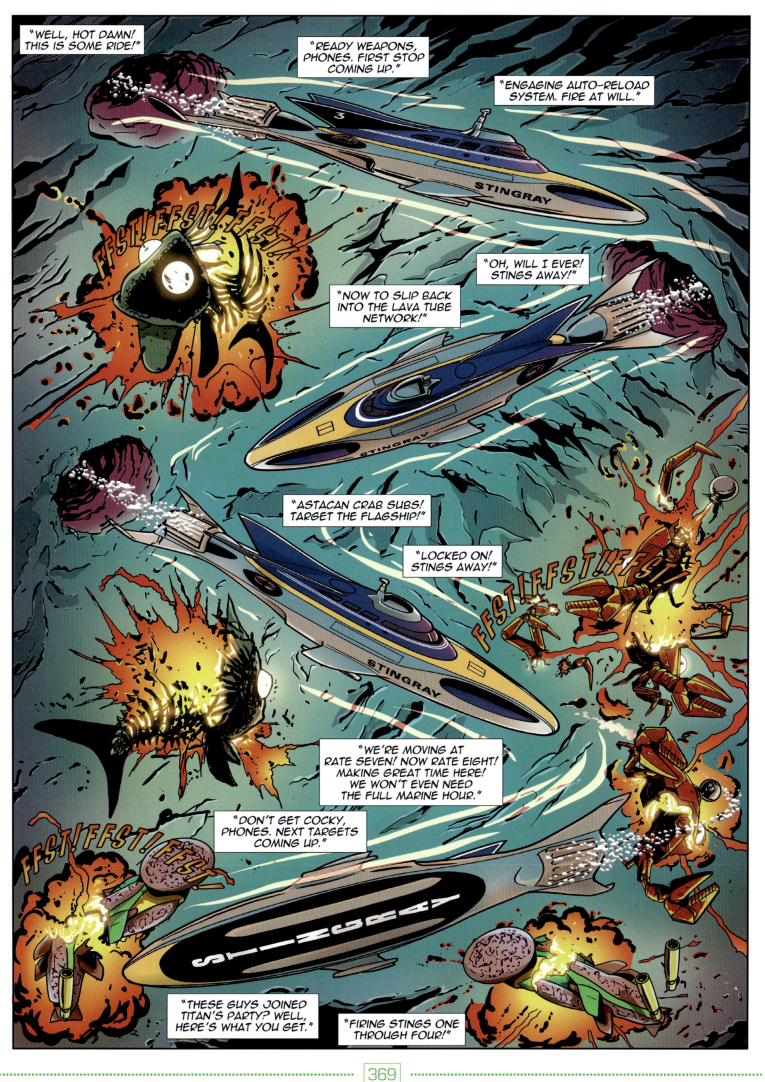

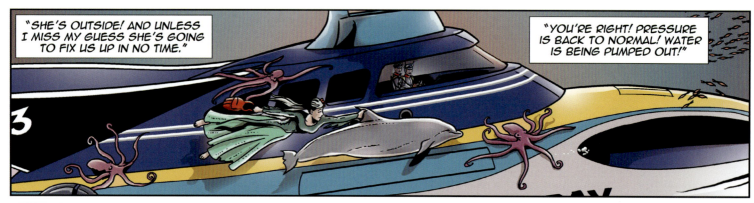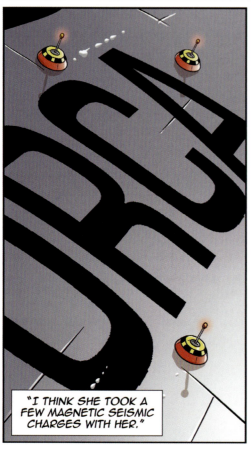

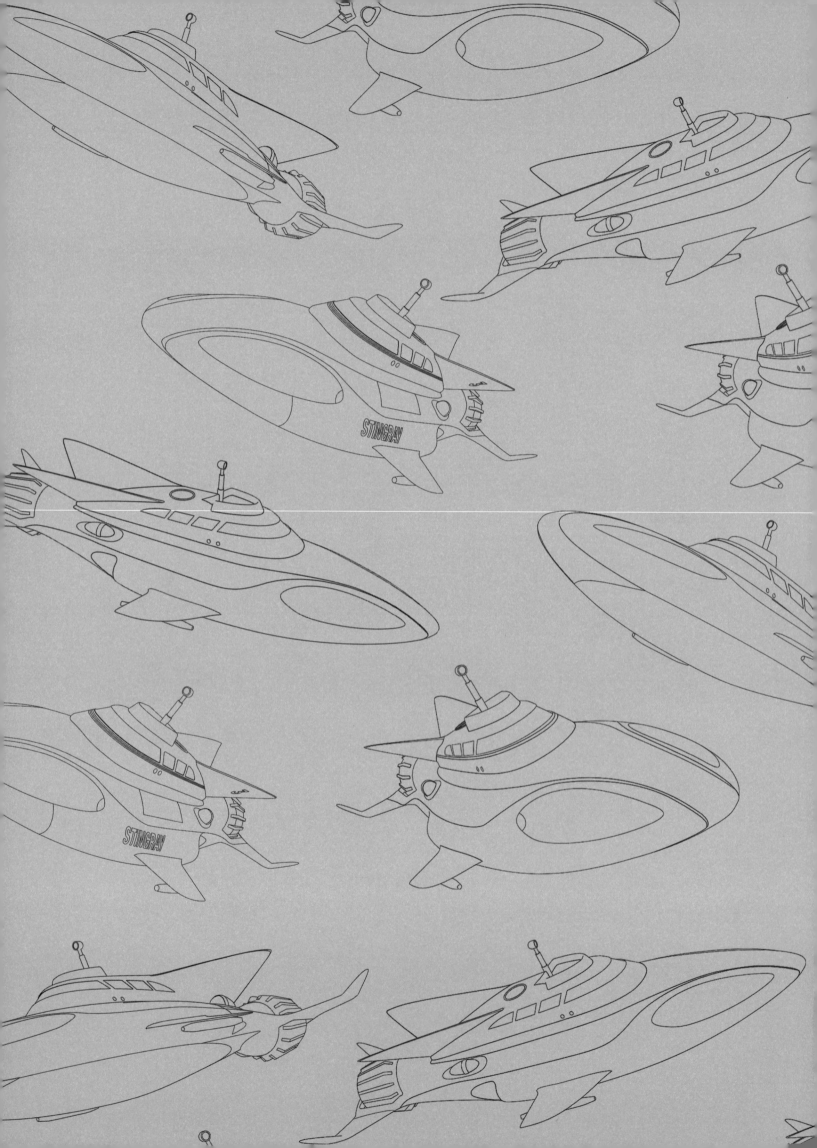